PUFFIN BOOKS

angels in training

Bestselling author Karen McCombie trained as a magazine journalist in her native Scotland before moving to London. After several years working on teen favourites *Just 17* and *Sugar*, she turned to fiction, with her first series, Ally's World, becoming an instant success. In total she's had more than seventy books published and translated around the world, and more than a million books sold.

Karen lives in north London with her very Scottish husband, Tom, her sunshiny daughter, Milly, a demented cat called Dizzy, and Biscuit, the button-obsessed hamster.

Find out more about Karen at:

www. karenmccombie.com

Books by Karen McCombie

ANGELS NEXT DOOR
ANGELS IN TRAINING

Don't miss the next book in the series!

ANGELS LIKE ME

angels in training

Karen McCombie

PUFFIN

PUFFIN BOOKS

Published by the Penguin Group
Penguin Books Ltd, 80 Strand, London WC2R ORL, England
Penguin Group (USA) Inc., 375 Hudson Street, New York, New York 10014, USA
Penguin Group (Canada), 90 Eglinton Avenue East, Suite 700, Toronto, Ontario, Canada M4P 2Y3
(a division of Pearson Penguin Canada Inc.)
Penguin Ireland, 25 St Stephen's Green, Dublin 2, Ireland (a division of Penguin Books Ltd)
Penguin Group (Australia), 707 Collins Street, Melbourne, Victoria 3008, Australia
(a division of Pearson Australia Group Pty Ltd)
Penguin Books India Pvt Ltd, 11 Community Centre, Panchsheel Park, New Delhi – 110 017, India
Penguin Group (NZ), 67 Apollo Drive, Rosedale, Auckland 0632, New Zealand
(a division of Pearson New Zealand Ltd)
Penguin Books (South Africa) (Pty) Ltd, Block D, Rosebank Office Park,
181 Jan Smuts Avenue, Parktown North, Gauteng 2193, South Africa

Penguin Books Ltd, Registered Offices: 80 Strand, London WC2R ORL, England

puffinbooks.com

First published 2014
001

Text copyright © Karen McCombie, 2014
Chapter illustrations by Madeline Meckiffe
All rights reserved

The moral right of the author and illustrator has been asserted

Set in 13/20pt Baskerville MT Std
Typeset by Jouve (UK), Milton Keynes
Printed in Great Britain by Clays Ltd, St Ives plc

British Library Cataloguing in Publication Data
A CIP catalogue record for this book is available from the British Library

ISBN: 978-0-141-34454-6

www.greenpenguin.co.uk

MIX
Paper from
responsible sources
FSC
www.fsc.org   FSC® C018179

Penguin Books is committed to a sustainable
future for our business, our readers and our planet.
This book is made from Forest Stewardship
Council™ certified paper.

*For Amy Smith — not forgetting
her everyday angel, Shimmer*

Contents

Freaked out and starstruck

I'm running, racing, breathless.

Nearly there.

Nearly at the very top of Folly Hill.

Nearly at the statue.

It's as if she's watching us coming.

'Yay – I win!' yells Pearl, slapping her hands on the marble plinth a split second before I do.

'Well done,' I pant, flopping my back against the ice-cold stone.

I was hoping that running up here this chilly Sunday morning would shake the thought, the secret, out of my head, but it's still there, rattling around.

I see Sunshine applauding us both, as she and Kitt go to sit on the bench just a little below us.

I glance away quickly, kicking at the frost-tinged grass with the toe of my ankle boot.

The thing is, my best friends don't know about my secret.

It's a secret that makes me feel guilty.

And confused.

Ungrateful too.

After all, a few weeks ago I felt lonelier than a wisp of cloud in a clear blue sky – till *they* turned up in my life, moving in next door, the mismatching foster kids of Mr and Mrs Angelo.

But I can't help the way I feel.

And I can't tell them my secret, cos the secret is about *them*.

It's this – they freak me out.

That's it.

My friends freak me out.

Isn't that tragic?

I mean, look at them – Sunshine, all calm and

willowy, her long, red-gold hair dancing in the buffeting November breeze.

Kitt, so super-smart, even if the pair of tight, dark buns in her hair make her look a little like a cute, girl-version of Minnie Mouse.

And dainty, giddy Pearl, with her white-blonde stubby plaits framing her perfect and perfectly pretty face.

All three of them are great, and they make *me* feel great (when they're not freaking me out). Actually, forget great, these three girls are *awesome*.

Ask anyone at school – when they're not busy gaping at them in wonder cos of their cute, kooky charm or their frighteningly casual cleverness in class.

In fact, it blows my mind that Sunshine, Kitt and Pearl actually like me.

Every now and then I have a moment: a moment, like I'm having now, when I can't handle the fact that we're friends at all.

It's just that I'm so ordinary, so un-special.

As for my friends . . . well, *this* is what my secret's

all about. *This* is the reason these great, awesome, extra-special girls freak me out: my friends happen to be angels.

Absolute angels.

For real.

'What?' Pearl suddenly asks, beaming at me, her breathing completely back to normal while I'm still panting like an elderly Labrador.

'Huh?' I gasp, shrugging at her.

'Is something wrong, Riley? You've got a sort of *thinking* face on.'

Pearl tilts her head to one side, her eyes darting about, trying to read my human body language.

Please don't let her guess what's rattling around in my head right now.

'It's nothing . . . nothing. Just tired myself out,' I lie.

Pearl's pale grey eyes are a little unnerving. I wish I had my camera with me; it's great to hide behind sometimes. But I left it in my bag on the bedroom floor – I was using it to take photos of the school

ukulele band for the newsletter on Friday. So instead I glance away from Pearl and stare up at the white statue looming above us.

Catching sight of the marble lady's familiar face makes my thumping heart rate start to slow, maybe because ever since I was small I've loved her. As a little girl I'd gaze at her clasped hands, her skyward stare, her flowing robes and towering arches of wings – and sometimes pretend she was my mum. (Is that dumb? Or just sad? Or totally understandable for a kid who never had the chance to get to know her mum for real?)

Whatever she was, the Angel was the most perfect thing I'd ever seen, and I'd curtsey to her, to this glorious figure that looks out over the valley, over the roads-and-streets tangle of our town.

All these years, all of my life so far, *she* was what I thought an angel should look like.

Not a twelve-year-old girl dressed in a cropped pink duffel, with long stripy socks and glittery baseball boots. Blowing bubblegum.

Pop!

'Sure that's all?' asks Pearl, cross-eyed and giggling as she picks a piece of the popped gum off her nose.

Pearl's new to bubblegum – Dot got her into it. My sort-of-stepsister has also introduced her to the delights of clapping games (once Pearl got over the worry that she was slapping and hurting Dot) and lemonade (the shock of all the fizzing made Pearl spit it out at the first bubbly sip).

I guess cos Dot's only five she doesn't question why our exciting new neighbours can sometimes be a little hazy about stuff *every* kid should have seen/done/experienced in their childhood. She's just way too excited at having a new playmate in Pearl in particular. Specially since *I* tend to spoil Dot's fun and roll my eyes at her a lot.

'Yeah, yeah, that's all,' I say, smiling shyly at Pearl, as I absent-mindedly scratch my head.

You know, being best friends with angels is like suddenly finding yourself hanging out with the

most famous teen actor or singer on the planet, only it's:

a) a *lot* weirder, and
b) something you can never talk to *anyone* about.

Actually, there are plenty of things I can't talk to the angels about.

I mean, if three *average* girls had moved into my old friend Tia's house, I could've asked, 'Where did you live before?' or, 'What was your old school like?'

If they were in a genuine foster family (instead of a magicked one), I could chat to them about their birth families, and what had happened to bring them to live with the human-but-oblivious Mr and Mrs Angelo.

But normal and ordinary questions don't cut it.

Instead I have huge, deep, brain-swirling, mind-blowing questions that I'd love to know the answers to.

Like, 'What *are* you exactly?'

Like, 'Where have you come from?'

Like, 'Why did you choose to help *me*?'

Over the last couple of weeks I *have* tried. But the three girls just laugh or look confused, as if I'm being silly or the questions don't make any sense to them. And I guess I'm way too starstruck and in awe of them to keep asking. (For now.)

Also, I think I'm maybe a *teeny* bit scared that their answers would completely freak me out . . .

'Riley?'

It's Dot. She's been hurrying after us, her skinny little legs struggling to keep up, her tied-back fair hair flipping and flopping *exactly* like a pony's tail.

She's clutching Alastair's lead in her hand.

Next to her is Bee – Sunshine, Kitt and Pearl's snow-white fluffball of a dog.

Bee is helpfully holding Alastair in his jaws.

(It's lucky that Alastair is a chunk-of-driftwood-pretend-pet and not a real animal, or we'd

be yelling 'Drop it!' very anxiously right about now.)

'What's up, Dot?' I smile at her, glad she's suddenly right here to distract me from my guilty, confusing and ungrateful thoughts.

'Do you have nits?'

'No, I do *not* have nits!' I reply, taken aback.

What's she on about?

Though I don't know why I'm surprised. Dot is an expert at coming out with stuff that makes you want to curl up and die. If there was an exam in Embarrassing Your Big-Sort-of-Stepsister In Public, she'd pass it with an A***.

'Why are you scratch-scratch-scratching, then?' Dot asks.

Suddenly, I'm aware that my fingers are burrowing in my muddy-puddle brown hair.

You know, something *is* tickling me.

But it can't be nits (shudder). Cos the tickling feels . . . it feels like it's *inside* my brain.

'You look like Bee when you do that,' giggles Pearl, watching me itch and scratch.

'She does, doesn't she?' Dot agrees, joining in the joke at my expense.

'Look, I don't know what it is, but it's *not* nits,' I say, addressing myself to Dot.

'Anyway, if I did have them, then you would too,' I add. 'It'd be your fault, cos you're always coming home with letters from your primary school saying they're going around.'

That shuts Dot up.

If there's one thing she hates more than homework/being nagged to brush her teeth/the boy down the street who's nicknamed her Spot, it's getting her hair treated for nits.

Whenever her mum, Hazel, brings out the dreaded, smelly hair treatment, Dot yells so much I worry that the neighbours will think she's being fed to wolves or something.

'*Whee!* Watch me!' Dot suddenly calls out, switching off from the conversation *she* started. (What's new?)

So I watch as she gallops off and throws herself happily into a cartwheel. But I guess cartwheeling on the frost-tipped grass with Bee and Alastair is a lot more fun than teasing me and risking future Torture by Nitcomb.

Argh, there's the tickle again. Or maybe it's more of a maddening prickle.

What's wrong with me?

Am I going to have to go home and Google my symptoms? '*Inner Head Prickles . . .*'

OK, now Sunshine and Kitt are looking my way. They can't think I have nits too, can they? I don't believe they even know what nits *are*.

I mean, all three girls must've had lessons or read some kind of guidebook about what to expect when they showed up on Earth from wherever. (Yep, another question I haven't had a proper answer to.) The thing is, they're ace at all our school subjects, but there are still some pretty big holes in their day-to-day knowledge. Last week, when Dot was playing with her yo-yo, the sisters ended up staring at it for

ages, mesmerized, as if they were watching someone scale the Shard without the aid of a safety rope.

So, no, Sunshine and Kitt probably *aren't* wondering whether or not I have nits. What's making them stare, then? What are they thinking?

Biting my lip, I give my head another scratch and return Kitt's stare. She's leaning on the back of the park bench, her chin in her hands, brilliant-blue eyes magnified by thick, black-rimmed glasses. (Will I ever get used to those intense Kitt glares?)

And Sunshine – Sunshine is standing up and walking towards me, her long legs like licorice sticks in her black tights and undone ankle boots. (Will I ever stop worrying that she'll trip over them one of these days?)

As Sunshine gets closer, it's the weirdest thing – the prickles and tickles inside my head get more and more maddeningly itchy.

She comes to a standstill, eyes locked on mine, and smiles.

'You're stopping me,' she says simply.

I haven't a clue what she means.

'Is she?' says Pearl excitedly, clapping her hands together. 'Wow, can you do that now, Riley?'

And then – *blam* – I get it.

The brain prickles-and-tickles – it's Sunshine.

She's trying to muscle her way into my mind.

'Please don't do that,' I burst out. 'It's as bad as reading someone's diary!'

I probably look pretty dumb, slapping my hands across my forehead, lamely trying to protect what's inside.

But I don't care; I'm too busy being hurt.

Hurt that Sunshine's done the seeking on me, trying to tune into what I'm thinking.

I mean, *yes*, she and her sisters came to my rescue when I was lost and lonely, which I'll never forget. And I really don't mind being a guinea pig for some of the skills they have to practise.

But not this one. Not when I have feelings I don't want on show.

Trainee angels may be awesome, but an ordinary everyday girl needs a little bit of privacy now and again.

'What's a diary?' I hear Pearl ask, but I'm still busy frowning at Sunshine and not about to answer her.

'I was only trying to see how strong you've become, Riley.' Sunshine smiles at me, her violet-blue eyes blinking, her cool fingers reaching up to touch my clasped hands.

And with her touch comes the warmth.

A sense of soothing hot water coursing over my hands, my face, my chest and back, as if I'm relaxing in a steamy shower instead of standing on a windswept hill.

'What do you mean?' I ask, letting her soothe me, letting my shoulders sink.

'Wow, your shine is strong, Riley!' she says, smiling at me, her eyes ever-so-slightly changing colour, like the swirls of oil on a wet road. 'That's brilliant. It means you don't need us any more.'

Those last words she said are like a punch in my chest.

Are they going?

Leaving?

Suddenly, the warmth isn't working any more. The thing is, I knew that was the angels' plan – they'd move on at some point, to someone somewhere who needed them more than I did – but I hadn't thought it would happen so soon.

Please . . . I didn't really mean any of that stuff about you freaking me out, I fret silently. *I'll make an effort not to be so shy; you can try out as many skills on me as you need to. Just don't vanish from my life!*

'Now you're strong, Riley, we can use all our energies to find someone new to help,' says Kitt, suddenly joining us, joining in the leaving speech.

They might think I'm strong, but *I* don't feel ready to lose my friends, not yet. And what about the promise they made, to help me find out more about my mum? I've been meaning to remind them about

15

that, just as soon as I get over my latest bout of shyness.

'We think we can sense a fading at school,' I hear Pearl say – which immediately makes me feel better. I mean, if the next person they need to help is nearby, then they won't be moving away anytime soon, will they?

Then – as the relief kicks in – I start fretting over who might be in trouble.

'Someone's stopped shining?' I ask, concerned. 'Any idea –'

'Hey, have you found any, Sunshine?' Dot interrupts, skipping up beside us again before I can finish my question.

'Any what?' Sunshine asks, the wind whipping strands of red-gold hair around her head like dancing rays of light.

'Nits!' barks Dot.

'No,' says Sunshine, letting her fingers fall from my forehead where they were still resting.

'Really? Oh well,' mutters Dot, as she ruffles the

furry head of Bee, who has conveniently positioned himself under her hand. 'Anyway, I'm bored. Can we do something? Can we have an adventure?'

'Yes, let's have an adventure!' Pearl agrees enthusiastically with Dot.

But she's looking straight at me.

In fact, all three angels are looking at me.

Their eyes have turned the exact blue of the sky above us.

Well, I guess I'd better try and feel as strong as they think I am, cos they might need me.

The angels have their powers, but who better to spot someone fading than a girl who's been there already?

A girl like me, who lost – and found – her shine.

Better, brighter, stronger?

One locket, two tiny photos.

On the left-hand side there's me, head down, smiling shyly. On the right is Tia, my far-away friend, beaming, laughing.

'Hey, night-night,' I whisper to her, aware that when it's morning here it'll be evening in New Zealand, which is home for her now.

I fasten the silver heart shut with a soft *click* and tuck it under my school shirt, then watch myself in the wardrobe mirror as I move on to my tie.

Not so long ago, the thought of Tia moving away, living on the other side of the world, leaving me – it was like a deep, burning pain. But that feeling has gone now – thanks to the three freaky girls who live next door in Tia's old house.

And what's special is that *I* was the angels' first: the first person they ever helped.

They somehow found me, my shine already dimmed because of losing Mum when I was a baby, fading further as I hovered in the dusky sidelines while Tia stood bright and beautiful. Fading dramatically fast when she and her family closed the door on 33 Chestnut Crescent and left for the last time.

'If a human's shine fades altogether,' Sunshine had told me, that day I'd discovered who and what my new neighbours really were, 'it can never come back. And that can leave you with sadness for all your life.'

Thanks to Sunshine, Kitt and Pearl, I'm SO much better, brighter, stronger than I was, I remind myself, trying to shake off the confused feelings of yesterday, up on Folly Hill.

With my striped tie now looped and knotted, I turn away from the mirror – and find I'm not alone.

Dot is in my room.

She's not doing anything loud or dumb or annoying, which is unusual.

Instead, she's sitting with her back to me on the edge of my bed.

The ears of her rabbit onesie flop forward as she stares intently at the only photo I have of my mum, in its mirror-edged frame.

I have a small but starring role in that photo. The bump under Mum's flowery dress – that's me, all snuggled and small inside her, while she stands on the top of Folly Hill, her arms flung wide, smiling up at the great wide sky.

'What if . . . ?' Dot mutters, squiggling to get comfy, runkling up my duvet.

I hold my breath, wondering what she's going to say.

Is she thinking – like I sometimes do – what life

would've been like if Mum hadn't died in the accident?

If the family living in this house had been just a threesome of me, Mum and Dad, instead of a quartet of me, Dad, Dot and Hazel?

Wow. *That's* a weird 'what if'. I can imagine life without Dot's mum, Hazel (no offence), but not Dot. What would I do without her bouncing around the house, entertaining and infuriating me? It would be quiet. Way too quiet.

'What if what?' I prompt her, as I tuck the skinny end of the tie into my shirt.

'What if our eyebrows were *under* our eyes instead of above?'

As Dot turns and blinks earnestly, I realize that:

a) she's just been using the edges of the mirrored photo frame to see her reflection, and

b) she's drawn upside-down eyebrows on her cheeks with something that looks worryingly like a felt pen.

'Dot! What are you doing?' I gasp, and rush round to grab a packet of wipes I keep on my chest of drawers.

'Just thinking of questions, Riley,' she replies, trying to wriggle away from my big (step)sisterly face-scrubbing. 'Miss Harris, my teacher, says we should always ask questions. It's a sign of a . . . a *something* mind.'

Scatty mind, in Dot's case, I think, relieved to see that the brown scribbles are coming off.

'You mean, an *enquiring* mind,' I tell her.

'Yes, that!' Dot agrees. 'Miss Harris says that having a *kwiring* mind is a good thing and that she wants us all to come to class with some interesting questions that we can talk about today.'

'Well, that's nice, Dot, but it's nearly time for school, and I think Miss Harris would also like you to come to class *dressed*.'

Never mind Dot's teacher, what about Dad? Hazel's on an early shift at the hospital today, and so it's his turn to drive Dot to her primary school.

22

I bet he'll be expecting her downstairs, all washed and in her uniform, any second now.

And all he's going to get is a bunny with unbrushed teeth and half an eyebrow to the left of her nose.

'Do you want to hear my questions, Riley?'

'Not really,' I say, with a final swipe of a wipe as I hustle Dot off the bed and out of my room.

'Well, here's one: *I* want to know why the Earth and moon and sun and stuff are all *round*. Why round? Why not triangles?' Dot asks, unfazed by my lack of interest as we cross the hall to her room, me with a hand on her fuzzy back. 'Then there's the eyebrow thing . . .'

'Yep, got that,' I say, having a quick look at my watch. Eek.

'. . . *and* I want to know how come some mums and dads give their children interesting names like Sunshine and Kitten and Pearl –'

Er, I'm not going to interrupt her here, but I'm pretty sure angels don't technically *have* parents.

(Something else for my list of mind-swirling questions.)

'– and not boring short names like Dot, which makes me sound like I'm *this* big.'

Dot pinches her finger and thumb till they nearly touch, while I ransack her wardrobe at high speed and throw her uniform on her polka-dot bed cover.

'Dorothea Madeleine Marshall,' Dad's voice booms from the doorway, 'you have practically the longest name in the world, and I know for a fact that you were called after your lovely and not-at-all-boring grannies.'

Dot scrunches her nose, thinking about that.

'And I *also* know that you're going to be late for school,' Dad continues, stepping into the room, 'and you're making Riley late too! Go on, Riley – scoot. Your friends are waiting for you outside.'

Sunshine, Kitt and Pearl are always waiting wordlessly by my gate on school mornings. Bee too, for that matter.

24

'Thanks, Dad,' I say, smiling up at him as I escape.

'By the way, Riley,' I hear him call after me as I thunder down the stairs. 'Keep meaning to ask – how does that dog of theirs do it? Make its own way back home after it's walked you all to school, I mean.'

'Well trained, I suppose,' I call back to him, though it's something I've often wondered myself. Specially when he shocks drivers at the busy junction on Meadow Lane by waiting for the green-man signal to cross.

Grabbing my blazer and bag, I pause just long enough to bend down and pat Alastair in his dog basket. I'm not totally mad; it's just a habit I've got into cos I know it'll make Dot happy. (And it makes me smile too, I suppose.)

'Hello,' says Sunshine, as I pull the front door closed behind me.

'Hi,' I reply – then realize she didn't say it out loud.

She likes to do that. To see if I can pick up what she's saying without talking, her lips moving fractionally. The skill is quiet words, and the girls use it to talk among themselves without being heard. (Useful for chats in class without getting detention.)

So I'm starting to catch what they're saying — getting better at reading lips these days, I guess.

Now I just need to get better at asking them stuff.

Hey, maybe I should be like Dot and set myself a target of thinking up a killer question for my friends today.

The problem is I'm just not sure how to pick only one from the flurry that's always swirling in my head.

Then Bee, padding fluffily by my side, gives me an idea.

No, I'm not thinking about Dad here, and his worry about how Bee finds his way home alone. I'm sure an angel-trained dog would have no problem with that. In fact, average, normal dogs can be capable of sniffing and navigating their way around too – with the exception of Alastair, of course.

'Aren't you ever scared that Bee might get run over?' I ask, thinking of the steady, lumbering stream of traffic on not-so-scenic Meadow Lane, just beyond the end of our road.

That's not my killer question, by the way. I'm working up to that.

'No,' says Sunshine, shaking her head, her hair tumbling like glowing amber ribbons, even with the jumble of pretty hairclips she uses to hold it back. 'Why would we?'

'He's very sensible,' Pearl adds cheerfully, smiling down at Bee, who seems to smile back. 'More sensible than us, actually.'

'But bad things can happen to sensible people – or dogs,' I say, thinking suddenly of my mum. 'A driver could be going too fast, not looking . . .'

As we turn into the growl and roar of the main road, I realize I don't know where Mum's accident happened. It could have been right here, at the

27

busy junction. Or outside her flower shop in town. It could have been down a dirt track on safari or on the racetrack at Brands Hatch for all I know. It's just one of the many questions I can never, ever ask Dad, since he never, ever wants to talk about her.

'Bee would still be fine, I'm sure,' says Sunshine, in that steady, reassuring way of hers.

'Unless he was distracted. Then the bad thing could happen.' That's Kitt, talking in her usual, blunt way. She's frowning, I notice, and the other girls notice too. They look concerned but say nothing.

I don't know what any of the girls are thinking (what's new?) and they often talk in something that sounds an awful lot like riddles to me.

But, as the green man at the traffic lights bleeps and we start to cross, I'm ready to come out and say what I mean.

'I know it wouldn't, but if something . . . something *bad* did happen, would you be able to bring Bee back?' I ask.

Yep, I want to know what sort of powers the

average angel has. What Sunshine, Kitt and Pearl *might* be able to do when they're fully trained, whenever that may be. (Spot *another* question I need to get around to asking.)

'No – we don't have skills to do that,' says Sunshine, stepping on to the safety of the pavement.

'Dead is dead.' That's Kitt again, *blunt* again.

'Oh, OK,' I mutter. So, even if Mum had been as lucky as me and had a guardian angel hovering around her, she still would've died. No one human or angelic could have brought her back to life.

The realization makes me sorry and sad for a second and a silence descends on us, though the traffic close by is pretty much deafening, same as the yells and chat of streams of students strolling or stumbling along the dead-end street that leads towards Hillcrest Academy.

'Oi, Riley!' A strangled sort of shout breaks through the din.

I glance around, but can't locate the voice.

'Riley!' it comes again.

'Look, it's that boy who talks to you,' says Sunshine, pointing a long, thin arm in the direction of what looks like a rugby scrum just up ahead of us on the pavement.

Sure enough, there's Woody in the middle of it all. Tall, goofy Woody Slater, who is in one of the other Year 7 classes, and who used to be my friend Tia's biggest fan. (Probably still is – I'm sure that's the only reason he talks to me.)

He's bent over in a headlock, while lots of Year 8 boys bundle on top of him.

'Are those bigger boys *fighting* him?' Pearl asks, sounding alarmed.

I can see why she thinks that and why Bee has run off towards the scrum barking and growling.

'They're not fighting; they're just mucking about. It's what boys do for fun,' I explain, sure that I'm right because of the lads' gruff laughter, and the fact that Woody has just extricated himself and is grinning as he gamely limps his way over towards us.

'That is a strange kind of fun,' mutters Kitt, scowling through her dark-rimmed glasses.

Human life must seem very, very peculiar to anyone on the outside.

Especially *boy* human life, which I don't get myself sometimes.

'So,' says Woody, smoothing his dark rumpled hair with one hand and bending his tall body down to pat Bee with the other. 'Going to the *News Matters* meeting at lunchtime, Riley?'

'Yes,' I answer him, a little confused. Why's he asking? It's only my second-ever meeting with the team, since I became photographer for the school's online news website. And Woody's not involved with it.

'I've asked to join.' He grins lopsidedly at me (or maybe he's just *all* lopsided after that wrestling session). 'They said I can come along to the ideas meeting this lunchtime; see how I get on. Thing is, I've got this GREAT idea that's going to totally blow them away!'

'Yeah?' I say, raising my eyebrows. 'What's that, then?'

'Not telling – yet!' he says, tapping his nose and winking at me, which I think is meant to make me all intrigued.

But, if he's expecting me to beg him to tell, he'll have a long wait.

I know a story that would make whatever Woody's got seem as exciting as an episode of *Peppa Pig*.

Could you imagine if I did an interview about that moment in the girls' loos a few weeks ago, when I found out that Sunshine, Kitt and Pearl were more than just my new, slightly kooky neighbours? That heart-stopping second when those huge wings unfurled in front of me, one looming, rustling pair after another?

Or if *News Matters* actually printed that photo I have on my pinboard at home?

'That's a pretty amazing effect,' Hazel had said, when she'd dropped off my laundry one day and

found herself entranced by the three blurs of white light in front of the statue on Folly Hill.

She'd had no idea what she was really looking at.

A trio of angels as they truly are.

'Anyway, catch you there. Yeah?' says Woody, zooming off after his thuggish buddies.

At the same time, Bee turns and ambles in the opposite direction, his bushy blonde tail whacking happily on my leg as he begins his homeward journey to Chestnut Crescent.

'So,' I begin, as me, Sunshine, Kitt and Pearl once again fall into step beside each other, 'what's the plan for today?'

Now the school gates are looming close, I'm pretty keen to know how exactly we're going to find whoever's fading.

The only problem is no one seems to know the answer.

Sunshine, Kitt and Pearl are all looking at me curiously.

'Um, the plan is we have science first thing?' Pearl suggests uncertainly.

'No, I was talking about the person who's lost their shine,' I reply, a little shy and awkward again. 'I just wondered what the plan was . . . to find them, I mean.'

'Oh, *that*!' giggles Pearl, as if magically tuning into someone's sadness was the simplest thing to do.

'You'll see,' says Kitt. Always the most serious of the sisters, her face, as well as her words, give nothing away.

'We'll show you,' whispers Sunshine – then I realize she didn't say that out loud.

She's used quiet words, or maybe she's sneaked inside my mind again while I wasn't looking.

Funnily, I don't mind; I'm suddenly buzzing with excitement, thinking of all the angels' skills.

When they were helping me, I didn't understand what they were doing, what was happening or why.

But this time – well, *this* time I'll be watching. And maybe even helping?

Written in red

I'm not sure if Mrs Mahoney is having way too much fun in the staffroom or if she's been abducted by aliens, but there's no sign of her yet.

Not that any of my classmates seem bothered about our registration session starting late, though.

Groups of girls are sitting around or leaning on the big library tables, chatting and giggling.

Groups of boys are doing much the same, with a few arm punches and lazy kicks at each other thrown in.

Meanwhile I'm sitting at the table nearest the library's check-out desk with just the people you'd

expect. Only they're doing something you might *not* expect.

Sunshine is pretending to read a book.

Kitt is staring at – but not seeing – the clouds outside the big plate-glass windows of the library.

Pearl is acting like she's daydreaming, twirling a pencil in the fingers of her right hand, as if it's a tiny cheerleader baton.

If anyone else in our class glances over at our table, they'll think my friends are doing nothing very much – but they'd be wrong.

I can see what's happening.

See, *there* – Sunshine's elbow is pressing against Kitt's arm.

Kitt is leaning back in her chair, with Pearl's left hand lightly resting on her shoulders.

They look like what they pretend to be – three foster sisters who are as close as best friends.

But I know the press of the elbow, the hand on the shoulder, are anything but casual.

Connected by those innocent-looking touches,

Sunshine, Kitt and Pearl are working together, making the skill stronger. They're seeking, quietly trying to tune into whoever's lost their shine.

It's as if I can almost feel what they're doing – there's the faintest vibration on the surface of the table where my hands are resting.

Wouldn't it be amazing if the person the angels are searching for is right here? In our own class?

'Hey, have you heard?' says Ella Brown, rushing into the library, blazer flapping.

'Heard what?' asks someone in the gaggle of girls all bunched round the back table near the non-fiction section.

'Well, Marnie Reynolds –'

'Who's she again?' another voice asks.

'Snooty-looking one in Y7A, with the dark bob,' yet another person explains.

There're a few 'Oh yeah!'s of recognition. I'm pretty sure I know who she is – Y7A is Woody's class, and I think I've seen him talking to her.

'Anyway,' Ella carries on, 'apparently Marnie

Reynolds is having a party at her house this weekend. *With no adults.*'

*Ooh!*s and *Aah!*s burble from the girls, and the boys start craning in, wondering what's going on.

'And guess where she lives?' Ella asks rhetorically, just about to tell us, you can sense.

'In one of those huge houses up by the golf course,' Lauren Mayhew butts in, using her best all-knowing and slightly bored voice.

No offence to witches, but Lauren is the closest I've ever been to one. She's the type of girl who'd be completely beautiful if she didn't ruin it by having the meanest look on her face at all times.

Right now she's lazily scrolling down the screen of her phone, her long blonde hair flopping over it. Either side of her are her cronies Joelle and Nancy, staring at whatever's so interesting on Lauren's display.

'So,' says Ella, trying to grab back control of her gossipy piece of information, 'I bet everyone'll be dying to get an invitation to that!'

'I wonder who's going?' asks someone.

'Us, for a start,' drawls Lauren, tossing her hair back and holding her phone up so the bunch of girls at the neighbouring table can read the texted invite she must've got from this Marnie girl.

People lean forward and make impressed noises, which only eggs Lauren on.

'Yeah, apparently Marnie can't *stand* her mum, so while she's away this weekend Marnie's decided to have this party – and doesn't care how wild it gets!'

There are more *Oohs* and *Aahs*, and Lauren grins slyly. You can tell she's loving having the insider information – but what she's said has niggled.

For one thing, how can it be true? No matter how bad Marnie Reynolds's mum is, it doesn't sound very likely that she'd leave her twelve-year-old daughter all by herself for a whole weekend. And how can someone not stand their own mother? Don't they know how lucky they are to have one at all?

But, hey, I don't want to seem like I'm hanging on Lauren's every – and possibly not true – word, so I turn quickly back to my friends.

'Getting anything?' I ask them, keen to know if the seeking has worked.

'Not sure . . . still scanning,' says Kitt, her eyes a darker, more intense, almost navy shade of blue as she concentrates. Sunshine doesn't lift her head, but I can just make out her eyelashes fluttering, trembling.

'Riley . . . what's a party again? I can't remember,' whispers Pearl, taking her hand off Kitt's shoulder as she leans over towards me.

'Pearl!' snaps Kitt.

A chastened Pearl quickly reverts to her position, hoping, I suppose, not to earn another cross on the skills chart that's pinned to the wall in their loft bedroom. The first time I saw it, I thought it was some kind of behaviour chart. I guess you could still think of it that way, only swapping various magical powers for promises to keep your room

tidy and not hide crisps in your pillowcase. (Those two are on *Dot's* behaviour chart.)

'A party,' I whisper, leaning closer to her, 'is where lots of people get together to chat and laugh.'

Pearl scrunches up her nose and seems confused.

'So, it's like this?' she asks, glancing dubiously around the library.

'Uh, no, not exactly,' I reply, though I get why she maybe thought that from my description. 'There's usually music –'

'I like music!' Pearl says enthusiastically, not spotting the dark look Kitt's throwing her.

'– and dancing,' I finish.

'And dancing's like *this*, right?' asks Pearl, taking her hand off Kitt's shoulder and wiggling in her chair.

'Pearl – concentrate!' Kitt snaps, reining her ditzy sister in again.

Pearl flops back almost sulkily and takes up her position again.

Just at that moment, a faint breeze seems to

41

stir – but the windows . . . they're all shut, as far as I can see. I give a little shiver, then see a drift of dust swirling in the glare of wintry sunlight streaming through the closed window.

But here's a funny thing . . . from where I'm sitting, I can see it's only swirling around *Kitt*.

'*Atchoo!*' she sneezes, making Sunshine stir. '*Atchoo! Atchoo!*'

I pass Kitt a scrunched tissue from my blazer pocket, but my eyes are on Pearl. She's biting her lip, trying not to smile.

Wait – was that *her*? The breeze, the drift of dust, Kitt's sneezing fit?

Pearl sees me watching and puts a finger to her lips, the universal sign for *Shh, keep my secret!*

Wow. I think she's just played a trick on her sister, using some strictly off-limits errant magic to get back at her for being annoying.

THWACK!

The library door is suddenly shoved open roughly and bangs against the library wall.

A wide-eyed Sanjay Kanwar rushes in, demanding attention.

'Get *this*!' he pants.

OK, even though I'm still reeling at Pearl doing something so mischievous, so un-angelic, Sanjay's got my attention – and everyone else's in the room.

Even Kitt and the newly awakened Sunshine are waiting to see what he has to say.

'There's a whole crowd of people in the boys' toilets downstairs,' he gasps. 'Cos there's this writing, see?'

'*What* writing?' asks Lauren, her face twisted with impatient contempt.

'On the four mirrors above the sinks . . . there's a word on each of 'em,' Sanjay babbles on. 'First one says *I*, second one says *AM*, next one is *WATCHING* and the last one is *YOU*.'

'*I am watching you*?' says Joelle, doing the head slide, arms folded, almost as contemptuous as her friend Lauren. 'Is that meant to be a joke or something?'

'Nah, it's not a joke – it's written in *blood*!' announces Sanjay, thumping his schoolbag down on the nearest table to emphasize his point.

Gasps and 'No way!'s rumble around the room. Lauren's friend Nancy slaps both hands on her mouth, her short, bitten, black-painted nails looking like cartoon rotten teeth for a second, which makes me want to do the opposite of my class and giggle.

'What . . . you *saw* this, Sanj?' one of the other boys shouts out.

'Not me, no,' Sanjay answers with a shake of his head. 'Couldn't get in – some teacher was there telling everyone to get out of the toilets and back to class. But the lads who'd seen it were all saying so.'

'*Blood!* Omigod, it sounds like a horror movie!' squeals Ella. She's paper-white, like she might faint.

'Maybe I should get down there and take a photo for the school newsletter,' I say, thinking about my camera tucked away in my bag, always at the ready.

'I'm guessing you're all talking about the silly graffiti in the boys' toilets?' says an authoritative

voice, and Mrs Mahoney, the learning resources manager, *click-clacks* into the room and strides to her position behind the big library desk. 'Well, let me tell you now, it was NOT written in blood. In fact, it was probably just a red whiteboard pen. And it's all wiped off now.'

Like Mrs Sharma – our regular form tutor who's off on maternity leave – Mrs Mahoney's smile is easy and wide, and today is untroubled by news of potential weirdness.

'But Sanjay said he heard –'

'Let's not get into Chinese whispers, shall we?' Mrs Mahoney says brightly to whoever was talking. 'I was chatting to another member of staff just now, and they said it was simply someone's idea of a joke. All right?'

Er, well, not really. There might be a certain number of shoulders untensing at Mrs Mahoney's explanation, but, to be honest, I don't think anyone in class – including me – is a hundred per cent reassured right now.

'*I AM WATCHING YOU . . .*' *It's not much of a joke, is it?* I think with a slight shudder.

I glance over to the angels, wondering what they've made of Sanjay's announcement and Mrs Mahoney's calming words.

Uh-oh.

Their eyes all match – irises the dark, brooding silver of pewter.

Whatever our temporary form tutor has said, it seems that something, somewhere in this school, is very, very wrong.

If only, if only . . .

Nine is the magic number.

That's how many skills there are; I know that much without asking, cos I've watched Sunshine, Kitt and Pearl practise all nine, and felt them being used on me too.

But right now I'd give anything to have – just for a minute or two – the ability to seek. I'd use that particular skill, of course, on the angels.

Cos they *were* freaked by the message in the boys' loos – I know they were. But will they talk to me about it? No. They've shut down completely, saying nothing about it at lunch just now.

'So you really don't have any idea what the red

writing means?' I try again, shoving my barely eaten pasta away from me.

'We're not picking up anything, Riley,' Sunshine insists again, her pleasantness infuriating me.

She doesn't know I could see them strengthening together a moment ago, using the power of three to boost the skill, same as they'd done in the library. This time, when I dipped down to grab my dropped fork, I'd spotted Pearl and Kitt's ankle-to-ankle link, and Sunshine's knee resting up against Kitt's.

Their radar is at high alert, I'm sure, but they're not about to let me understand or let me help.

Which only makes me worry more. Is it something so big they think it might frighten me?

'We're only searching for the fading,' Kitt reassures me.

Who knew angels could fib? Back in the library, I saw all their eyes change colour, which always happens when their powers begin to pulse. From Sunshine's violet-green gaze, to Kitt's cool blue, to

Pearl's pale grey; they're all switching to that dark, brooding shade – the blackest of rainclouds mixed with the sheen and shine of dark metal. That definitely didn't mean nothing.

If only I could seek, if only I could see inside an angel's mind.

But which one?

Kitt's too serious and sharp; Sunshine's too calm and in control to let me sneak a peek. But Pearl . . . *she's* the one who struggles with her skills the most, who lets things slip, who leaves silver glitter fingerprints where she shouldn't, who magics up drifts of dust motes to punish her sis.

Yes, of the three angels, Pearl is definitely the closest thing to a flawed normal person.

If only –

Uh-oh . . . I spot the time on the dining-hall clock and know I have to be somewhere. Whatever strangeness is going on, whatever the angels aren't saying, it'll have to wait.

*

'Good to see you, Riley!' says Mr Edwards, the ICT teacher, as I scurry into his classroom.

'Oh, hello,' I reply, shaking thoughts of otherworldly weirdness out of my head.

It seems I'm not the first to arrive for the *News Matters* meeting.

There's Mr Edwards, obviously, since he's the newsletter editor-in-chief – which basically means he lets the team use his room and computers, and checks all the stories before they're published. (During the last meeting he told us that an editor once ran a competition for the best caricature – and *News Matters* nearly went live with a doodle of the music teacher wearing a T-shirt that said *Loser* on it. Thanks to Mr Edwards, that image didn't make it to the webpage. *Or* win the competition.)

And today, apart from Mr Edwards, there's Daniel Jong from Year 10, who's the current editor and super-enthusiastic, plus feature writers Hannah Hollister and Billy Wright – both in Year 9 – and Ceyda Dogan from Year 8.

They all give me a wave from the corner, where seven chairs are set out in a circle.

Behind them on the wall are prints of a few cover/opening pages of *News Matters*, plus blow-ups of the team's favourite photos from the last issue. My face will flush pink when I say this, but each of the photos is *mine*.

There's the image of Woody holding Mrs Sharma's new baby, the two of them mid-wail. (The baby's muffiness was genuine; Woody's wasn't.) The others are a selection of the photos I took when Year 7 went to the Wildwoods Theme Park a few weeks back: girls' feet flying and flailing from the Swinging Monkeys chair ride; boys goofing around in the endless queues; Lauren Mayhew freaking out at the cobwebs and 'spiders' that fell on her during the Haunted House ride. (Thanks, Kitt, though only the four of us know that was down to you, and not a technical malfunction!)

'We're talking about ideas for the next issue,' says Daniel, as I slink shyly into one of the two free seats.

Don't ask me to come up with one, I plead silently. My head's been too full of awesome angels, tricky questions and fading victims to mull over feature ideas.

'Hannah's thought of interviewing the teachers about their own schooldays,' says Billy, sounding really keen on the idea.

'We could ask them to bring in their old class photos, which would be funny,' Hannah adds. 'Then we thought that you'd photograph them as they are now, Riley.'

'How about we get them to dress up in Hillcrest Academy ties and shirts, and take them in the same pose as their *old* photos?' I suggest, suddenly all fired up and forgetting to be shy, forgetting my frustration with the angels.

'Brilliant!' says Mr Edwards. 'And Ceyda also thought that –'

'Sorry I'm late!' yelps Woody, clattering through the door, all long legs and gelled spikes of dark hair draped over his forehead. 'But it's worth it – wait till you see what *I've* got!'

I'd forgotten that Woody was trying out for the *News Matters* team today. He's flopped easily into the one spare chair and acts like this is his fortieth meeting instead of his first. It's amazing to see someone who's the exact opposite of me – totally confident and sure of himself in front of people he doesn't know.

'Sounds intriguing!' says Mr Edwards, raising his eyebrows so they peek up above his glasses.

After rifling in his inside blazer pocket, Woody pulls out his phone and, from all the flipping he's doing, I'm guessing he's going to show us either a text or a photo.

'So has everyone heard about what happened in the boys' toilets this morning?' he asks, without looking up.

There's a rumble of interested 'Uh-huh's and 'Yeah's.

'Well, check *this* out!' he says, having found what he was searching for and gleefully holding out his mobile.

'What is it?' asks Billy, who's leaning in from the side but can't get a good view.

From *my* position, I can clearly make out white tiles, four mirrors . . . and red writing. It does look a little like blood, with those dollops and drips here and there. But as Mrs Mahoney said, someone could've mocked that up with arty use of a whiteboard pen, I suppose.

'It says, "CAN YOU SEE ME?" That's *another* message, isn't it?' gasps Ceyda, holding her hand to her throat.

'The first one was "I AM WATCHING YOU",' Hannah mutters.

'Exactly.' Woody nods.

'So someone's sneaked into the boys' loos again?' I say, squinting at the screen.

'Ah, but this time it *wasn't* in the boys' toilets – it was in the *teachers'* loos, right beside the staffroom,' Woody tells us with relish.

'What were you doing in the staff toilets?' Mr Edwards asks him, sounding puzzled.

54

'I wasn't *in* them,' Woody replies. 'Well, not at first. I just saw a crowd milling outside, heard what was going on and sneaked in for a look before anyone could stop me. I *did* get a detention from Mrs Zucker but it was worth it!'

'Hope it's not going to happen in the girls' loos next!' says Ceyda.

'Wow – would be *way* too spooky,' murmurs Hannah, biting the nail of her thumb.

'OK, let's not get excited here,' says Mr Edwards, holding his hands up for calm. 'So the joker's struck again – but that's all it is.'

'How can you be so sure?' asks Woody.

'Because I'm a teacher, and I've seen plenty of practical jokes before,' Mr Edwards replies.

'Yeah, funny stuff like locking people in the stationery cupboard and chucking their sports kit on the roof of the bike shed,' says Woody. 'This is different. This is pretty dark, don't you think? Like we're all being watched . . .'

'Maybe it's someone with a grudge?' Billy suggests.

'Who says it's a some*one*? What if it's a some*thing*?' says Woody.

Everyone freezes, even Mr Edwards for a nanosecond.

'You mean, like . . . like a poltergeist?' says Daniel.

A Mexican wave of shudders reverberates round our little circle.

'Whoa! Stop right there,' says Mr Edwards. 'There's no poltergeist, all right?'

'But it would make a great story, wouldn't it?' says Woody. '*Everyone's* talking about it.'

I don't know what idea Woody had on the way to school, but you can tell by the gleam of excitement in his eyes that this morning's happenings have blasted whatever it was *well* into a trailing second place, for sure.

'A stupid scribble or two by some idiot does NOT make a story, guys.' Mr Edwards laughs good-naturedly.

'Yeah, but I bet you a million pounds it'll happen again,' says Woody, as he stuffs his evidence (and

phone) back in his pocket. 'And when it does we *have* to write about it.'

I suddenly realize that Woody's talking like he's already part of the team, and everyone sitting in the circle – including me – seems so hooked on what he's saying it's like he's passed some invisible test.

'How do you spell *poltergeist*?' asks Billy, starting to scribble in his notebook.

'N-O,' says Mr Edwards very definitely.

But no matter how sure Mr Edwards is about this being the work of a trickster, I can't help feeling a chill ripple all down my back.

Though I don't know why the idea of a poltergeist has unnerved me so much – it's not like I even believe in ghosts.

But then a fortnight ago I didn't believe in angels.

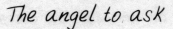

The angel to ask

THE NINE SKILLS:

- *SEEKING: tuning into someone's thoughts or feelings*
- *QUIET WORDS: talking with no sound*
- *VIRTUAL STROKING: infusing someone with a sense of happiness (starting with a touch, but doing it from afar)*
- *WARMTH: stopping a person panicking with a sensation of cascading warm water spilling over them*
- *SPRINGING: making someone tell you what's on their mind, without them meaning to (like a truth drug)*

- *CATCHING: seeing JUST into the future – phones about to ring, people coming round a corner, etc.*
- *SPIRIT-LIFTING: cheering someone up by letting them relive – just for a few seconds – a treasured memory*
- *TELLING (the second-strongest skill): giving a person an insight into something that's happened to them, like watching snatches of the bonus DVD of their life*
- *REWINDING (the strongest skill of all): the ability to stop time and unravel it back to a minute or so before*

If a guardian angel HAD been looking out for Mum on the day she died, I think, as I look at the words I've scribbled in the back of my homework notebook, *then surely rewind would've worked?*

Lost in thought and chewing the top of my pen, a sudden noise makes me jump.

'Wake up, it's a *beautiful* morning!'

That's Hazel I can hear, singing a snatch of some song.

'How are you, my angel?' she calls out, the door opening.

To Dot's room across the landing, that is.

Dotty is nothing like an angel. It's not that she's naughty; it's just that she's more likely to stab a too-small dressing-up tiara into your head than lay hands on it to release the warmth. And, instead of helping you regain your shine, she's more into helping herself to a handful of dry Cheerios from the packet if no one's looking.

'I'm FINE, Mummy!' I hear Dot yell, before she clatters into my room without a knock.

I'd be grumpy if anyone else did that, but Dot is a special case. I like being interrupted by her randomness.

'Do you have any wishes, Riley? You can have three,' she announces, skipping over to me in her fairy nightie. Dot's waving her coordinating wand, which she might have slept with because the points of the stars are looking a bit bendy.

I quickly shove my homework notepad under my

pillow and do a thinking face for her, as if I'm taking her offer *very* seriously.

Of course, if she was the real thing – a true, teeny fairy – *these* would be my wishes:

1. I wish I was less in awe of the angels, so I could ask more questions about who and what (and why?) they are.
2. I wish I could find out more about my mum, without upsetting Dad.
3. I wish I knew who the next person in need of angelic help was.

And, if I could wangle a *fourth* wish, I'd wish for yesterday's school prankster to be caught quickly. I couldn't sleep last night for thoughts of ghosts and ghoulies and poltergeists hovering and hiding round every corner of Hillcrest Academy.

'Hurry up – I need a wee-wee!' the fairy demands.

'And I need any washing you have, Riley,' says

Hazel, standing in the doorway with a half-filled laundry basket.

You'll notice there are no snatches of songs and sunshiny words for me. Just requests for dirty clothes and casual questions about how I've slept and how my day's been, in her efficient nurse's voice (since that's what Hazel is). It's not as if me and Hazel have a terrible relationship, but it isn't exactly what you'd call cosy and close. I guess if you imagine everyone living in this house as one of those Venn diagram thingummies, you'd have me and Hazel in separate circles with Dad and Dot in the overlapping middle section.

'Sure,' I reply, and scuffle in the corner of the room for the T-shirt and jeans I dumped there the other day. 'Here.'

'Thanks,' says Hazel, with a pleasant-but-not-totally-genuine smile. 'Your dad's making beans on toast right now, so it's about five minutes to breakfast. OK, girls?'

I say yes, but the fairy doesn't.

As Hazel bustles off, I turn to see what Dot's up to.

And it isn't good.

'Dot – that's mine!' I say, hurrying over to grab the notebook that she's slid out from under my pillow. Honestly, I can't trust her to stop noseying around my stuff at the moment.

'Actually, I want to be called Dorothea Madeleine all the time now, cos it's more interesting,' she announces, untroubled by me snatching my notebook back. 'So what *is* all that stuff? It looks like spells!'

'It's just some ideas for a creative writing thing,' I lie, tearing the page from the binder and scrunching it up in my hand. 'But it's rubbish really.'

With her five-year-old attention span, Dot is bored by the time the aimed paper ball clangs into the bin by the door.

'Miss Harris gave me a merit for my very interesting questions yesterday,' she trills, as she

hippetty-hops over to my window, all thought of loo desperation suddenly forgotten.

'Well done, Dot,' I tell her, as I now gather up my schoolbooks for the day. I'd've scored *minus* three merits for my lack of astute questions yesterday, if anyone had been keeping an eye on me.

'Dorothea Madeleine,' my sort-of-stepsis corrects me, as she squashes her nose against the cool glass window. 'Mr and Mrs Angelo are really nice, aren't they, Riley?'

I'm guessing Dot's watching our next-door neighbours right now, but I'm too busy searching for my other school shoe to go and look. Sarah and Frank Angelo do seem nice, though, and I find myself thinking about them sometimes. There they are, just a regular, normal couple who've fostered in the past, with no idea that some unknowable forces have deposited three extremely unusual foster children on them.

'Aw, yuck! What are they doing *that* for?' Dot suddenly groans, which nudges my curiosity enough to make me hop over to her, while yanking the found shoe on.

'They're only kissing!' I say with a smile, as Mr Angelo goes to move the wheelie bins out for the refuse collection, and Mrs Angelo heads off to work.

'Yeah, but it's *disgusting*,' says Dot, wrinkling up her nose. 'Don't you hate it when my mum and your dad do it?'

'Well, I – I guess I don't really mind,' I answer vaguely, though it does bug me a bit. Mainly because it makes me wonder what it would've been like to watch Dad and my *own* mum kissing. Oh, to have the luxury of being disgusted by that . . .

'Hey, Riley – look!' says Dot, swiftly shifting to something else that's caught her attention. 'Look at what's happening to Pearl!'

Uh-oh.

Pearl is holding a stuffed black plastic bag destined for the wheelie bin. But – unobserved by her foster parents – she has a flurry of butterflies dancing

65

around her head and shoulders. Pearl's looking at them in wonder as they land on her hair, on her shoulders, on her free, outstretched arm.

'She has this new perfume,' I say quickly. 'It smells just like flowers. Now go and get dressed before breakfast. Hurry!'

I grab Dot by her fairy-wanded hand and practically drag her out of my room and deposit her by the door to her own bedroom.

'But where are you going? Can't you help me with my woolly tights, Riley? They get in a tangle . . .' she bleats as I thunder down the stairs.

'I'll be back,' I call behind me. 'Got to ask Pearl something about homework.'

As I hurtle out of the front door with a hurried yelp of 'Back in a minute!' – aimed in the general direction of Dad at the toaster and Hazel at the washing machine – I know I have to stop Pearl before she's seen.

'Hi, Mr Angelo, just got to speak to Pearl,' I pant, as I zoom by him on the pavement.

'Call me Frank!' he says cheerfully, parking the black bin where it needs to go.

'Oh, hello!' says Pearl in pleased surprise when I stop breathless in front of her, sending the startled butterflies spiralling into the air.

'That thing . . . there,' I try to say, sounding anything but clear. 'Making butterflies appear in winter –'

'Oh! The bag smelled so bad – I just wanted something pretty to look at while I was holding it,' she explains.

'– or making Kitt sneeze yesterday,' I carry on. 'You know you can't do that sort of stuff.'

Pearl's smile fades and she looks crestfallen.

'You sound just like Kitt . . . but no, I suppose I shouldn't.'

I hate to spoil her fun, but I know from watching and listening to the angels that any kind of errant magic – the misuse of the skills – is wrong, for two reasons.

It weakens the angels' power for the tasks they

need to do, and, more importantly, it puts them at risk – they could be *spotted*.

And it's not the first time Pearl's done it. One time in the library, her fingers dreamily played with the dried, faded petals of some roses in a vase, totally unaware that her touch was bringing the flowers back to life, back to full bloom. Then there are the fingerprints she leaves behind, stains of fine, silvery glitter on doorknobs and taps, and trailed along walls when she's daydreaming.

It's the reason there're so many crosses on her chart in the loft.

What will it mean for her if she keeps scoring worse than the other angels?

I guess that's another question I'm too shy to ask. Or am I?

Maybe sweet and ditzy Pearl – the angel that's most like a normal, imperfect girl – is the person who might answer my questions for real.

Ready, steady, jump

BRINNNNNNNNNGGGGGGGGGGGGG!!!

'That is a *bad* noise,' says Kitt urgently, looking at me to explain another small gap in her normal-world knowledge.

All around us, students are doing one of two things – panicking, or giggling.

But whichever they're doing, they're all heading the same way – for the nearest exit.

'It's the fire alarm,' I tell my friends, glad that it's gone off now we've just finished lunch, instead of later in class.

Whenever we have a drill during a lesson, there's always an uncomfortable scramble and jarring of

elbows as we squash through the door, no matter how much our teachers yell, 'Quickly but carefully! No jostling!'

'There's a fire?' says Sunshine, seeming confused.

She turns her head this way and that, her flame-coloured hair tousling around her as I lead them the right way.

'Maybe, or maybe it's just a test, to make sure we know how to leave the building safely if there was a real emergency.'

'So this could be a *real* emergency?' Pearl suggests nervously as crowds of kids surf past us.

'It's not,' Kitt suddenly says, her now navy-blue eyes dark with concentration, seeking out some sense of the situation.

'So it's a drill, then,' I say with a shrug, as we follow our fellow students out into the fresh air.

'It's not that either,' Kitt tells me very definitely.

I don't want anyone to see the colour of her eyes, since they're not her usual sky blue, so I steer my three friends over to a low wall round the nearby

flower beds. It's close enough to our class's assembly point, but far enough away for no one to take much notice of us till Mrs Mahoney arrives to do a head-count.

Just in time – Sunshine's eyes are darkening too.

'Quick, face me!' I tell them, so that Sunshine and Kitt look my way. (And realize, with surprise, that I'm taking control of the situation.)

Pearl's not acting the same as her foster sisters, though. Instead of becoming still, going inside herself, she is hurriedly scanning the organized chaos and the teeming crowds all around us.

'Pearl . . . concentrate,' Sunshine says softly.

'But –'

'*Pearl!*' Kitt says a little more insistently.

Pearl hasn't heard or has chosen not to listen; she's stepping into the throng and is gone.

'You stay here – I'll get her,' I tell Sunshine and Kitt. I've just caught sight of Pearl's stubby blonde plaits as she weaves between bobbing waves of identical blazers.

I hurry after her, muttering quick ''*Scuse me*'s, and then practically stumble over two hunkered-down girls surrounded by a circle of onlookers.

'I don't know what's wrong with her!' one of the onlookers is saying, sounding panicked.

'I think she has that thing . . . what do you call it again? When you can't breathe properly?' says someone else.

One of the girls on the ground is panting and wheezing. It's Marnie Reynolds.

Pearl is the other girl. She must have been doing some seeking of her own and found Marnie in trouble, and is now crouched down beside her, smoothing her hands across Marnie's sleek, dark, bobbed hair.

She's calming her with the warmth, of course.

And, of course, *I* know what's wrong with Marnie. Having a nurse in the house has its downsides – we have to watch every hospital telly programme going, even if it's just so Hazel can moan about how unrealistic it is – but it does mean I can spot a medical condition when I see one.

'Do you have an inhaler on you?' I say, getting down on my knees and talking directly to Marnie.

Marnie nods, her breathing already easing slightly thanks to Pearl.

'In my bag,' she wheezes.

I grab the backpack next to Marnie and rummage through, quickly finding her asthma pump and handing it to her.

Marnie's tiny nod is thanks enough before she concentrates on taking deep, holding breaths from the inhaler.

'Is she going to be all right?'

'Will she be OK for her party?'

'Should we call an ambulance?'

'You don't think she'd *cancel* her party, do you?'

'Is this happening cos she was stressing out about the fire alarm?'

Questions and comments burble above us, but, like Pearl, I'm just concentrating on Marnie.

'OK, people, can we back up a little and let

me through, please?' I hear our PE teacher, Mrs Zucker, call out. 'How are we doing, Marnie?'

Mrs Zucker crouches down beside us, gently pushing Pearl's hands away, which is OK, as her job is done.

Marnie is now more herself, and begins to tell Mrs Zucker that – as someone suggested – panic about a possible fire had brought on her asthma attack.

Me and Pearl – we're listening, but, like the other girls, we do as Mrs Zucker asks and step away, then find ourselves suddenly standing with Sunshine and Kitt. They're both staring intently at their sister.

'Is it *her*?' Sunshine asks, without a sound.

Those quiet words send a thrill rippling through me.

It's Marnie. *That*'s what Sunshine means. She and Kitt think we've found the next person who's lost their shine. Isn't that funny . . . Pearl sometimes seems the most careless and least dedicated of the angels and yet she's the one who –

'Riley! C'mere!'

My elbow has been grabbed.

'You've got to see this – for *News Matters*,' Woody urges, yanking me, dragging me away from the throng.

With the jumble of students blocking his view, I don't think he's even aware anything was wrong, that one of his classmates was ill back there.

'See what?' I ask, stumbling reluctantly after him, tripping over feet and dumped schoolbags.

The thing is, I like Woody, but I've got mixed feelings about him since yesterday's *News Matters* meeting. It's cos of the photo he showed everyone on his phone. It was good, really good, and that's my problem, since –

'Just hold on – it's inside,' he interrupts my thoughts, aiming for an open door that leads into the language block.

'Hey! I'm not going in the building!' I tell him, trying to wriggle free. 'Are you deaf? There's been a fire alarm.'

'Riley, it's fine,' he tries to reassure me. 'I just heard Mr Bradley telling Mr Thomlinson that it's another hoax. Mr Thomlinson said he's just waiting for all the classes to assemble and then he'll make an announcement that everyone can go back in.'

I guess it *is* OK if the site manager has told the deputy head that it was just some kind of false alarm.

'But, if we go in there, *I* won't be at the assembly point with the rest of my class,' I try to explain to Woody. 'And Mrs Mahoney will go crazy at me if –'

'Look, Mr Edwards will sort it out with her,' Woody insists. 'You've *got* to do this for the school newspaper. Who else can take the photos, except you?'

That last bit swings it for me. My problem with Woody was this – I was asked to be in charge of photography for *News Matters* when I had zero confidence, zero shine. Taking photos, being with the angels . . . they'd both helped stop me from fading. I guess I was worried Woody might take that away from me, whether he knew it or not. Seems like that was the last thing on his mind.

'Right – show me,' I say to Woody, as I grab my camera from my bag.

'Great! It's along this way,' Woody says, bounding through the open door and lurching right, with me at his heels. 'Check it out!'

I nearly crash into Woody's back as he stops dead, splinters of glass crunching beneath his shoes, beside a smashed and activated fire-alarm button.

'It's not the button,' he tells me, his face flushed with excitement. 'Look here!'

My instinct is to point the camera first, and it's only as I focus on the image on the display that I see it.

Red writing, small and scrawly, just underneath the plastic casing of the alarm button.

DID I MAKE YOU JUMP? it reads.

'Yes, you did.' I mutter my own quiet words, as my shaky finger presses *click* – and my heart *thud, thud, thuds*.

77

Bittersweet and blue

The angels love being up high.

It's why they like Folly Hill as much as I do.

It's why they all chose to share the loft next door rather than have a bedroom each.

It's why they persuaded – possibly with the use of magic – Mr Angelo to build them a treehouse in the huge chestnut tree almost as soon as they moved in.

We're there now, after school, hunkered down in our great wooden nest. As it's getting colder these days, Mrs Angelo has given us a bunch of old cushions and blankets to snuggle up with.

Away from prying eyes (and ears), it's the

perfect place for an ordinary, real-life girl to talk to her *extra*ordinary angelic friends about what exactly is going on with all things super-strange at school.

Well, it would be, if we didn't have company.

'My name is Dorothea Madeleine Marshall,' announces Dot, scrambling up the ladder and on to the mostly level floor of the treehouse, followed by her best buddy, Coco.

Sunshine, Kitt and Pearl stare at Dot, possibly wondering why she's just introduced herself to them, since they all know each other already.

'Yes, it is,' Sunshine says in the momentary silence after my sort-of-stepsister speaks. Sunshine is always very polite.

'She's fascinated by names at the moment,' I try to explain. 'It was something she was talking about in her class.'

'My mummy and daddy named me after my two grannies. One was born in Greek and one wasn't,' Dot explains proudly (and badly).

'And *my* mummy called me after an old lady that invented perfume,' Coco chips in with *her* story.

She means the famous fashion designer Coco Chanel, I suppose.

'Why are you called *your* names?' Dot demands, looking directly at Sunshine, Kitt and Pearl.

'We chose them, of course,' Sunshine says with an easy smile.

'We named ourselves after things we liked,' Pearl adds happily. 'Sunshine is so beautiful, kittens are lovely and pearls shine so prettily. And Bee –'

Uh-oh. Since when have babies named themselves?

Sunshine and Pearl don't get it, but *Kitt* does. I can see the instant worry and panic in her eyes, as the two other girls make it stunningly obvious that they're not normal.

'Er, giving yourself a new name – it's a foster-kid thing,' I fib on the spot, wondering how I can elaborate on the lie some more.

But I don't have to.

'Oh, OK,' Dot says with a carefree shrug, happy enough with that explanation, just as it is. Thank goodness for five-year-olds having the attention span of a brick.

And then she floors me.

'What about you, Riley? Why did your mummy and daddy call you *your* name?'

'I – I don't know,' I answer her, suddenly realizing I have no idea.

Why don't I know?

Was Riley a name that meant something to my parents, or did it come pinging into their minds out of the blue? Was it Mum's idea more than Dad's? But then I might've expected her to name me after a flower – she was a florist, after all.

Thoughts rattle around my brain, but I try to ignore them as I struggle to give Dot more of an answer.

'I suppose I should try to find ou–'

'OK, bye, then!' Dot trills, already bored and

ready to move on to the next bit of fun. 'We're going to play with Bee and Alastair.'

Dot and Coco clamber down the ladder and within seconds I can hear them explaining to the dogs (well, one dog and a glorified twig) who is going to be who in a game of doctors and nurses.

Still, apart from leaving me waffling in mid-sentence, Dot impressed me there with her ability to ask what's in her head without hesitation.

Maybe I need to channel some of that right now.

'So what do you think this is all about?' I ask the angels, taking my camera out of my bag and showing them the image of the red writing again. They only saw it for a second at the end-of-day bell – when I explained I'd have to go and download it into the *News Matters* folder on the computer in Mr Edwards's room, and that I'd meet them at home later.

'We don't know, Riley,' says Sunshine, her face as

serene and calm as ever as she pulls a blanket up over her long legs, tucking it round the waist of her denim dungaree dress.

It's so frustrating. There's definitely something unsettling going on at school – apart from Marnie and her fading – and, out of everyone I know, Sunshine and her sisters are the best qualified to work out what that something is.

Only they don't seem to want to, or at least they don't want to tell me if they *do* know what's happening.

'Woody thinks it might be paranormal activity,' I say, trying to nudge a response out of them.

'You mean not normal, not *human*. Is that right, Riley?' Kitt asks, pushing her thick-rimmed black specs further up on to the bridge of her nose. She's blinking fast, her razor-sharp mind processing ideas, thinking unknowable thoughts.

'Like us . . . but *not* us?' Pearl mutters, looking worried.

Yes, like you, but not you, whatever you are, I think,

remembering that my friends are still a mystery to me.

'That isn't possible,' Kitt says, ever certain, ever practical.

'But with Riley our sensing was clear, and this time it's not,' Pearl frets, admitting to worries I hadn't expected her, or her sisters, to have. 'Everything seems buzzing, confused.'

'We're still learning, Pearl,' Sunshine quickly reminds her. 'All we need to do is stick together and focus and everything will –'

'Or we could just ask for help,' Pearl suggests.

'Pearl!' Kitt snaps, her eyes blazing.

'Ask who, ask what?' I say, my curiosity making me unexpectedly braver, stronger. Questions, questions, so many questions.

'Pearl means that we need to ask more of our skills, to help us move forward,' Sunshine says too quickly.

She's covering up, I think, covering up for Pearl being careless and saying something she shouldn't

have. In fact, I don't just think it – I know it. Pearl's face is pinched now – her mouth a tiny, startled 'o' of shock – realizing she's made a mistake.

'There's nothing to worry about, Riley,' Sunshine says in her best soothing voice.

But her soothing doesn't work, cos once again I feel freaked out by my friends.

It seems like there's so much they're aware of and so much they keep from me.

It's not just what's going on with Marnie or the red writing, the angels haven't helped me find out anything more about my mum. A knot tightens in my tummy; perhaps they can see into the past and know something that will hurt me or make me too sad.

I'm not aware I'm being studied till Pearl says something out of the blue.

'She's thinking about Annie.'

Pearl must've broken into my thoughts just now, without my permission, without me sensing her seeking.

I should be cross, but at the sudden mention of Mum – the surprise of Pearl using her name – all my indignation instantly drops away.

And maybe it's my own fault that Pearl tuned in on me. Perhaps I have some kind of aura that only the angels see. Perhaps mine lights up brightly every time Mum comes into my consciousness.

'I – I just want to know more about her,' I say simply, finally finding a question I can ask without getting myself in a knot.

Sunshine, Kitt and Pearl, in spite of the uncertainty fluttering between them a few seconds ago, now merge into one unit, leaning into one another, turning their luminous, silvery gaze on me.

It's the most nerve-jangling, skin-tingling experience I've ever had – part fright, part thrill.

'Come here . . .' Sunshine says softly, ushering me closer.

I hesitate for a second, then give in, letting myself lean over, lie down and curl up in the comfy cushion of knitted blankets on Sunshine's lap.

My eyes closed, I feel three sets of cool fingers rest on my head, shoulders, back and arms. Thirty tingling points of pressure that send pulses radiating through me, soft waves of energy easing into my body.

And the pulses . . . they turn into a heartbeat, slow and steady.

A murmuring, gentle voice, singing . . . singing what? Ha – it's just some silly but oh-so-familiar nursery rhyme.

I don't just *hear* the voice. The vibrations of it rumble against me, and I feel warm and protected and loved.

My cheek is against her chest.

The smell of her is roses.

Her song fades away and she kisses me on the head, lips and breath tender and soft.

'Everything will be all right, my little Riley . . .' she murmurs, she soothes.

'RILEY! DOT! TEATIME!'

The sudden shout of Dad's distant voice jars me out of the cocooned memory.

'Riley?' Sunshine's voice comes into focus as she helps me sit up. 'Are you OK?'

'Why are you wet here?' Pearl asks, dabbing away a tear that's coursing down my cheek.

'I – I'm fine,' I fumble, lost for words.

By the puzzled looks on all their faces, I can tell I've disappointed the angels. They wanted to give me a gift, a spirit-lift to let me have that snapshot of myself, small and bundled in a cuddle with my mum.

They thought it would leave me beaming instead of blue.

How funny, I think to myself. *A minute ago I felt as if I could never understand the inner workings of an angel. And now the angels have found that they can't always understand the bittersweet feelings of a sad-but-happy, ever-so-ordinary girl like me.*

'Dot, can you get out of the way, sweetheart? I just want to watch the news for a second,' says Dad, straining to see round the stripy vision standing in front of the TV.

88

'Uh-uh,' says Dot, folding her arms across her chest.

'What's up? Do I need a password?' Dad asks, sensing a stand-off.

'No,' says Dot, giving her head a shake.

'Oops – I forgot to say please, didn't I?' Dad tries again.

'No.'

Dad scratches his chin, stumped.

'Didn't I say enough nice things about your leggings and T-shirt?'

Dot has been skipping around the house for the last few minutes showing off the new clothes Hazel's bought her. They *are* nice, though they'd be better worn apart – all those stripes at once are enough to give you a migraine. Or maybe I just happen to have a killer headache after a confusing day of surprises, shocks and visions.

Now that my dishwasher duties are done, I've just joined Dad and Dot in the living room, flopping down on the sofa, next to Dad.

'Nope – it's not that,' Dot says flatly, still not budging.

Dad turns and mouths at me, *Riley, help!* which makes me smile.

And, as I'm quite an expert at understanding the randomness of my little sort-of-stepsister, of *course* I help him out.

'She's not answering anyone unless they call her Dorothea Madeleine,' I remind him.

'Ah, yes!' Dad now nods sagely. 'I forgot she's got a sudden fascination for names. Hey, Dorothea Madeleine, could you shift your bum out of the way and let me watch my programme?'

'Stuart! That is a rude word. You are a bad man!' Dot giggles, and launches herself at my dad.

Dad gives a pained 'Oof!' as she piles into him, but then he wraps an arm round her in a restraining hug and Dot quickly nuzzles into his side.

At the same time, his other arm encircles *my* shoulders and I'm happily pulled into a hug too.

And as we sit there all cosy on the sofa together –

bookending Dad – Dot says something that makes me love her more than I do already.

'Stuart, why did you and Riley's mummy call her Riley?'

Out of the blue, she's asked my question for me!

I sense the arm round my shoulders tense slightly. Holding my breath, I wonder how Dad's going to respond. I stopped talking to him about Mum a long, *long* time ago. Even though I was only little, I saw that the very mention of her hurt him way too much.

'Well,' Dad begins, doing his best to sound as chirpy as he came across a second ago. 'We, um, happened to see an exhibition –' there's a little crack in his voice there, giving away the fact that he's not as chirpy as he's pretending to be – 'by a famous artist called Bridget Riley.'

'And you called her Riley after the lady cos you liked her paintings so much!' Dot says excitedly, bouncing up on to her knees at the discovery of the origin of my name.

I feel like doing it too, but instead only celebrate by allowing myself to breathe again.

'Well, after looking around her paintings, we realized we weren't *particularly* fans of her art, no,' Dad explains. 'But we did like the name Riley, so when *this* madam came along soon after –' he squeezes my arm and gives me a look that makes me want to melt, it's so raw and sad – 'it seemed . . . perfect.'

'Why didn't you like the lady's paintings? What were they like?' Dot demands, not seeing that Dad is having a moment of the bittersweet blues himself.

'Stripy. She painted lots of stripes,' he tells Dot, his voice cracking just a little.

'Stripes! I LOVE stripes! Can you show me on the computer, Stuart, can you?'

'Come on, *I* will,' I tell her, shoving myself up off the sofa, and holding my hand out for her to grab on to.

I'm buzzing from this small but crucial piece of my history and need to get away from Dad before

he sees the happiness I'm struggling to keep from him, since it'll clash badly with how I suspect *he's* feeling.

But, before I go and check out my namesake, I do one small thing.

I kiss my dad on the forehead, and hope he understands that it means thanks a million.

The same, but not the same

Things I know about my mum (a very short list):

- Her name was Annie.
- She died in a road accident when I was a baby.
  (Of course I know this much.)
- She had long fair hair.
- She had a beautiful smile.
- She liked to wear flowery tea dresses.
  (These three points I know from staring at my one photo of her.)
- She ran a florist's shop called Annie's Posies, which was right beside the train station in town.

*(The old lady I met on Folly Hill a few weeks ago –
she told me that. She told me because she said I looked
exactly like her . . .)*

- My dad loved her so, so, SO much that he
  can't bear to talk about her.
  (Sadly.)
- I am named after an artist who painted pictures
  that make your eyes go funny.
  *(Thank you, thank you, Dorothea Madeleine, for
  finding that out for me.)*

'Riley! You are *not* going to believe this!' Woody's
eyes are wild, his grin wide – and my meandering
thoughts of Mum are instantly banished.

It's lunchtime on Wednesday and we've both
arrived at the door to Mr Edwards's room from
different directions. I'm holding the sandwich
I bought from the dinner hall, and Woody is holding
a jumbled pile of white A4 sheets in his hands.

'What?' I ask, frowning.

'Hold on – we should show everyone!'

And, with that, he shoves the door open with his shoulder, and we see the rest of the *News Matters* team already settled in the usual circle of seats, notepads in hand.

'Hi, guys,' Mr Edwards calls out to us. 'Just been chatting about that photo you downloaded yesterday, Riley.'

'We should definitely do something about the red writing, after the fire alarm yesterday,' says Daniel, the editor. 'Even Mr Edwards agrees now that it's all anyone is talking about.'

Mr Edwards holds up his hands, surrendering to the story.

'Forget that! They're all going to be talking about *this* now!' Woody holds up the wodge of paper, then passes us a sheet each.

I'd thought at first that the paper was blank, but now I see there's actually something written in a small red font in the centre of the page.

'*YOU CAN LOOK, BUT YOU WON'T FIND ME.*'

It's only when everyone's eyes are turned my way that I realize I've read the words out loud.

'There are *hundreds* of these,' Woody now starts explaining. 'You know the student printer by the maths block? It was still churning them out when I left just now. People are picking them up, passing them around like crazy.'

'OK, that's it. We *have* to have this as our main story,' says Daniel, his eyes gleaming. 'Let's get started on it now. Ceyda – can you write about what's happened so far?'

'I could research poltergeists, for a sidebar,' suggests Billy.

'And I'll talk to the head or one of the deputies to get their opinions,' says Hannah.

'Great,' Daniel replies, scribbling in his notebook, while Mr Edwards grudgingly nods his agreement, obviously still a bit uncomfortable with the whole school-weirdness topic.

'If you want, I could go back to the maths block and do a vox pop,' Woody suggests.

From the way Daniel's eyebrows shoot up you can tell he's not about to say no.

'Great – and Riley, you go with Woody to take photos.'

And so with no time to think, let alone speak or plan, I'm zooming to keep up with Woody's long legs as he sprints along corridors, through swinging doors, and bounds up sets of stairs.

'We've got to be quick – the afternoon bell goes in a few minutes,' he tells me, as we approach huddles of chattering students hovering round the still-rattling printer.

I get busy taking photos of the scene, only vaguely aware of what Woody says next.

'I'll grab those lads first, and *you* line up someone else for me to talk to, yeah?'

Help . . . I don't want to do that! I mean, I'm less shy than I used to be, but I'm still pretty useless when it comes to talking to people I don't know. My mouth – my *brain* – tends to go on strike. I'm just

about to say so when I notice that Woody is already chatting to the boys.

Also, I've spotted a familiar face, standing on her own, a hand covering her mouth as she reads the sheet clutched in her hand.

'Um, Marnie? Are you OK?' I walk over and ask, worried that the shock of the latest weird message might make her feel bad again, same as the fire alarm did yesterday.

'This is so spooky,' says Marnie, not really paying attention to me. Her face is white against her dark hair – though I don't hear her wheezing, I realize thankfully.

'Yes, it is,' I agree, suddenly feeling a bit bumbly now I'm speaking to her. I mean, yes, so I passed her an inhaler in the playground yesterday, but that hardly makes us friends. The state she was in, Marnie probably wasn't even aware of who the helping hands belonged to.

In the moment's silence, I take a deep breath,

working up to asking her if she'll be interviewed by Woody, when I spot the angels further along the corridor, perched on the windowsill.

They're sitting completely still, apart from Pearl's feet, swinging back and forth in her stripy socks and glittery baseball boots.

Sunshine and Pearl smile, while Kitt mouths some quiet words at me.

'*Keep Marnie there,*' she is wordlessly whispering. '*We're going to spring her.*'

So the angels *do* need me after all. They need me to somehow hold Marnie Reynolds's attention while they get her to speak her mind, whether she wants to or not.

And whatever she says, whatever clues she gives about what's troubling her, I'll remember every word and report it back to the angels.

This is it. I have to be brave and strong and useful.

'I'm – I'm Riley Roberts, I'm in Y7C,' I say, thinking I should properly introduce myself, if

we've got so much in common – if she's a girl going through what *I've* gone through.

'Yeah, I know you,' says Marnie, gazing up from the A4 sheet.

Her brown eyes suddenly look glazed, as if she's been hypnotized. Which she pretty much has, I suppose, if the angels' skill has already taken hold.

'I think you're in the same class as Lauren Mayhew. Are you her friend? I think you were there yesterday when my asthma was bad.'

The disconnected words and thoughts Marnie Reynolds has been holding in her head are spilling, spilling, with no gaps for me to respond.

'What *are* these messages appearing at school? I don't like them. They're creepy. I wonder who's doing them? It better not be anyone I've invited on Saturday. I hate the way everyone is acting like my friend, just cos they want an invitation to my party. Is that the only reason you helped me yesterday? Is that why you're talking to me now? Just so I ask you to my party too?'

101

'No!' I say sharply, hurt that Marnie thinks I'm so shallow, when actually I'm trying to help her – not just with her asthma but with her lost shine too.

But that one harsh word of mine – it acts like a sudden antidote to the springing. Marnie blinks, uncertain of what she's said, uncertain why she's even *talking* to me since she doesn't really know me.

'Hey, Marnie,' Woody says chattily, bounding over to join us. 'Do us a favour and give us a quote about the messages for the newsletter, yeah?'

'Uh, OK, why not?' Marnie agrees, sounding now a bit offhand, a bit snooty.

'Great! Riley, do you want to grab a photo first?'

'Do I have to?' says Marnie, glancing at me from the corner of her eyes, as if I'm toxic.

'Yes, you *have* to,' laughs Woody, spinning her round to face me. 'How about holding up the sheet and looking scared?'

'How about I don't?' she says back, without a flicker of a smile.

102

'How you are is fine,' I mutter, wanting to get this over as quickly as Marnie obviously does.

I lift my camera, and in the display I see a girl with her nose in the air, as if she's looking down at me through the lens.

As I press *click*, I'm filled with a sudden sense of doubt.

Is this confident, possibly vain, not particularly grateful or friendly person really losing her shine?

Or am I just disappointed that this fading girl doesn't realize I want to help her?

Photo taken, I gaze in the direction of my friends to see their reaction to Marnie – but the windowsill is empty.

In the corridor there's only a jumble of students, all *so* caught up in the latest red-writing message that I bet none of them will notice the solitary white feather spiralling down against the backdrop of the cloud-filled sky outside . . .

*

103

The afternoon is made of elastic, undercover chatter about the eerie photocopies ebbing and flowing, lessons stretching to double their normal length, the ring of the end-of-day bell never coming.

I stare across at one or other of the angels as they sit upright and attentive in class, putting their hands up for every question, getting every fact right, of course.

And then – after something just short of forever – the *briiiiiingggg* of the bell releases us and I can finally talk *properly* to the girls about Marnie.

But, nope, it isn't that simple. Coming out of science, I am grabbed by Daniel Jong, the *News Matters* editor, keen to hear how the vox pop has gone.

It is another elasticated five minutes till I can politely wriggle myself free, and so here I am now, hurrying out of the main entrance, and hoping my friends will still be waiting for me.

At first glance, it doesn't seem like they are. Everyone's made a speedy exit, apart from a few

trailing, chatting girls, a couple of boys lazily kicking a ball back and forth, a knot of Year 7s by the gate.

But at second glance I see a snow-white blob of fluff being fussed over by some breakaway members of the Year 7 knot, and I assume that if Bee is there, then Sunshine, Kitt and Pearl can't be far.

'No way! You *have* to have something new for the party!' I hear a girl roar, as I sidle into the outskirts of the group.

At the centre are Sunshine, Kitt and Pearl, and from the babble of crossover chatter I pretty quickly realize they are being congratulated on being invited to the party that *everyone* is desperate to go to.

When did that happen? It must've been when I was with Daniel just now.

It's funny, but my heart sinks not just a little, but a lot. I don't even know Marnie, and I'm not sure I even like her that much, but it still hurts when you realize you're not on a list that plenty of other people are. Especially when those people include

your best friends. Though *of course* Sunshine, Kitt and Pearl would be invited – they're pretty, smart, interesting and unusual.

Unlike me.

Sorry-for-myself tears well up out of nowhere. I'm so embarrassed that I pretend to look in my bag for something (good for hiding the eyes).

'Where's that stupid book got to?' I mutter, rifling through my stuff, before heading back towards school to 'look' for the not-missing-at-all book that I never had in the first place.

Not expecting anyone to have noticed, I jump when I feel the hand on my arm as I walk back through the sliding entrance doors.

'What's wrong?' says Pearl, tilting her head, her eyes scanning, scanning for clues about why I'm upset.

'I just forgot something,' I tell her, keeping up the pretence.

'No, you didn't,' Pearl says, with the sweetest smile.

I let my shoulders sag and decide to say something closer to the truth.

'It's silly, it's nothing. I'm just . . . a bit muddled right now.'

Pearl nods, blinks her blonde-fringed eyes.

'Yes. I'm just a bit muddled right now,' Pearl repeats.

I really like Pearl, but I wish she wouldn't do that. It's like that irritating game Dot plays, where she copies everything you say, even down to 'Stop, please, Dot!' (' "Stop, please, Dot!" Hee hee hee . . .')

And then, as Pearl continues to smile at me, I realize something very, very surprising. Pearl *isn't* trying to *copy* me. I think she's actually trying to *tell* me how she feels right now.

'You sometimes don't feel good enough,' Pearl adds, tilting her head the other way.

'Yes,' I say simply.

'Sometimes *I* don't feel good enough.'

I'm slightly in shock. I've seen Kitt lose her temper (dramatically) and Sunshine get frustrated.

I've seen Pearl slip up, with her thoughtless, carefree, tiny trails of magic. But I hadn't expected that one of the angels might need someone to talk to. Someone non-angelic, I mean.

Only a couple of days ago, I'd wondered if Pearl was the most approachable angel, and here she is approaching *me*. It seems she's the same, and yet not *quite* the same, as her very special sisters.

'Do you mean –' I pause and lower my voice, aware that there're still staff milling around in the nearby school office. 'Do you mean that you're worried about the skills? About not being as good as Sunshine and Kitt?'

All the questions I have for the angels start rattling around my mind again.

I mean, with the skills – how will they be able to tell when they *are* all good enough at them?

It's hardly like Sunshine, Kitt and Pearl will get a certificate in the post. Or a handshake from the head at assembly, like *we* do if we get a hundred merits for good behaviour.

'My skills don't glow like theirs,' Pearl says frankly. 'You should see –'

'WOOF WOOF!'

With a *swoosh* of sliding doors, Bee runs into the entrance hall and jumps his front paws excitedly up on to Pearl.

'Oh!' she gasps in surprise.

'What's this?' calls out one of the office staff. 'No dogs in here, please. Come on – get it out, girls!'

'Of course,' I say, shooing Pearl and Bee back into the playground – where a smiling Sunshine and a brooding-looking Kitt are standing waiting for us. (I quickly brush a few sparkly fingerprints from my blazer so Pearl doesn't get into *more* trouble.)

All my questions, including a new one about how skills 'glow', will have to wait till I can get Pearl on her own again.

Though when will that *ever* happen?

Unravelling and rewinding

It's really getting too cold – and too dusky – to hang out in the treehouse after school.

But it's so private up here (unless Dot's with us).

Special too (unless it's raining).

And the view . . . wow. Over the rooftops you can see the daylight fading over the town in one direction and the sun setting over the Angel and Folly Hill in the other.

All of that makes it hard to think about hanging out anywhere else, even a cosy bedroom or loft.

So I gather a blanket tighter round myself and carry on with our conversation.

'Wait . . . you *made* Marnie Reynolds invite you to her party?' I ask, checking that I've got this right.

While I was chatting to Daniel Jong earlier, it seems that Kitt used a little twist of magic to wangle an invitation to the party.

'Well, I put the idea into Marnie's head,' Kitt admits, as she wraps a woolly scarf round her neck.

Apart from the actual skills, the angels seem to have a few other tricks up their blazer sleeves.

'Kitt saw that it was already there – in Marnie's mind – to invite us,' Sunshine is quick to reassure me.

'She just hadn't mentioned it yet,' says Pearl.

'The party will be a chance for us to be close, to see why her shine is fading,' Kitt explains.

When Kitt says 'us', she means her and Sunshine and Pearl. Not me.

Kitt sees the party as work, I guess, not fun, which is why she didn't think to add me to Marnie's guest list.

III

What the angels can do for a person is incredible and important – just look at the change in *me* if you want proof – so I understand how Kitt would see it that way.

I just wish I didn't care so much.

'Angry with someone?' we hear a voice call out from down below.

It's Dad's voice.

And now I can make out the shrill-but-happy yelps of Dot and Coco as they run from Dad's car to our house.

Wonder what Dad's on about? And who he's talking to?

I put my gloved hands on the wooden ledge of the treehouse and peer over.

'No – I'm not angry, thankfully! Just trying to figure out which of these is *leaking*,' laughs Mrs Angelo, as she whacks the pillows she has pegged to the washing line. 'I keep finding white feathers everywhere!'

'Bet you it'll be one of those mysteries you can

112

never solve,' Dad jokes, hovering before he follows Dot and Coco into the house. 'Bit like the socks that go missing in the wash.'

Well, er, not exactly like that, I think to myself with a secret smile.

The angels join me, getting up on their knees to peer down at our parents, foster or otherwise.

There's Dad's dark-brown head, going grey at the sides. There's Mrs Angelo's light-brown hair, bobbing as she laughs at Dad's remark. One other head is down there – it's snowy-white and turned up to face us.

Both my dad and Mrs Angelo seem to notice and look up at the same time.

'You lot are like a bunch of wise owls up there!' Dad remarks with a broad grin. 'Maybe *that's* where the feathers are coming from!'

You're getting closer, Dad, I say silently to myself, as Mrs Angelo laughs some more.

'By the way, Riley,' Dad calls up to me. 'It's fish

fingers for dinner tonight. Dot – sorry, *Dorothea Madeleine* – and Coco requested it.'

'Oh . . . OK,' I shout down, trying not to show my lack of enthusiasm, though I can't help it if fish fingers are my *least* favourite teatime option.

'Actually,' Mrs Angelo butts in, 'would Riley like to eat with *us* tonight? I've made a huge pot of spaghetti bolognese, so there's plenty –'

'She'd love to,' Pearl calls down on my behalf.

Of course I'd love to.

I've never been to the Angelos for dinner; I've never really talked too much to the girls' foster parents.

It could be interesting. And the more chances I have to hang out with Pearl – maybe even get her on her own – the better, since sweet, imperfect Pearl is the one person – OK, *angel* – who might answer my questions.

So, half an hour later, I'm sitting in the white dining room of 33 Chestnut Crescent, feeling a little shy as I share the table with five people, two I don't know very well, and three I do (though sometimes I'm not so sure about that).

'Anything interesting happen at school?' asks Mrs Angelo, as she passes round a bowl of garlic bread.

'We got invited to a party on Saturday!' says Pearl.

Yeah, but technically, we didn't ALL get invited to a party, did we? I think a little gloomily.

'How lovely. Your first party since we moved here. And nice to hear some news at last!' Mrs Angelo adds, smiling, teasing.

'Absolutely,' Mr Angelo says jovially, beaming a big smile at the angels in his midst. 'Riley, I hope you're better at telling *your* parents about what's happening at school than this lot. Though of course we know what people your age are like – full of secrets kept from us boring grown-ups!'

At his words, Mrs Angelo looks fondly at the many, many framed photos of former foster children on the walls.

I don't suppose any of them were quite as extraordinary as Sunshine, Kitt and Pearl, or had a secret *quite* as jaw-dropping as theirs.

'It's just my dad, actually – Hazel is his girlfriend. She and Dot moved in about a year ago,' I explain.

'And your mum?' asks Mr Angelo. But he says it in a matter-of-fact way, which I like. If someone acts all concerned, it makes me uncomfortable, like I might want to cry or something.

I bet Mr Angelo said it that way cos he and his wife have had to hear pretty sad and bad stories from all the kids they've fostered over the years. They've probably learned through experience just what to say and how to say it.

'She died when I was a baby. She was in a road-traffic accident,' I answer just as matter-of-factly.

Oh no.

As soon as I say it, I instantly wish I hadn't.

What if Mr and Mrs Angelo mention something to Dad over the garden fence? *Riley was telling us about her mother . . . we're so sorry to hear she died so tragically.*

Can you imagine? He would absolutely *hate* that. I mean, if Dad can't face his own daughter talking about her mother, he's not going to love semi-strangers next door getting all chatty about it, however kindly meant.

The angels sense my stress, I'm sure – they're all staring at me, trying to tune in.

I'm about to let them when Mrs Angelo speaks.

'That's terrible,' she says. 'It's so upsetting when you hear about young lives lost. Just the other day I read in the local paper that there's been a campaign for years now to improve the crossing further down Meadow Lane, near the library. Apparently it's a real accident blackspot. The worst case was a young mum who was knocked down and killed there more than a decade ago and *still* nothing's been done –'

As soon as the words are out of Mrs Angelo's mouth, I can tell that, like me, she wishes she hadn't said them.

Because, like me, she's just made a mental note of timings and probability.

Of course, another young mum might have been in a fatal traffic accident around the same time as my mother, but that would be a bit of a coincidence, wouldn't it?

And, as the realization sinks in, it feels as if someone's just punched me in the chest, making it hard to think, speak or breathe.

'Riley?' says Mr Angelo, concerned all of a sudden, leaning towards me. As his outstretched hand reaches towards my arm, I feel a soft but steady trembling that's got a sound to it, a noise like a hiss on a wire.

Mr Angelo's hand is hovering in mid-air, as still as if he'd been turned to stone.

It's unnerving to lift my eyes and see his gaze frozen on me, unblinking.

And, when I turn to the other side, Mrs Angelo's eyes are fixed on me too, wretched with apology, but her body is rigid, the gloopy spaghetti gently unravelling from her fork and slipping back down on to the plate.

'What's happening?' I ask the girls.

I'm finding it hard to look directly at them. The effort of doing what they're doing is lighting up the room, their own eyes like six piercing, silver-white laser beams.

In a panic, I hurry over to the windows and pull the curtains shut so no neighbours – especially my own family next door – get a glimpse of what's going on.

'You're upset, so we're going back,' murmurs Sunshine, as the two other angels soundlessly mimic her words. 'You don't have to worry about things you wish you hadn't said, or why.'

'But I'll still be able to remember what Mrs Angelo just told me, about that accident?' I check, realizing I'm witnessing a memory rewind in full flow.

'If that's what you want,' Sunshine says, while Kitt and Pearl mouth the sentence.

'I do,' I say very definitely, very surely.

I've just added another – not very happy but vitally important – fact about Mum to my short

what-I-know-about-her list, and the last thing I need is to let it slip away.

Blinking as the light intensifies, I feel a deep warmth that's immediately replaced by a temperature dip – and the room returns to a normal level of brightness, the overhead light doing all the work.

Mr and Mrs Angelo smile again, coil pasta on to forks again, chit-chat again.

'Absolutely! Riley, I hope you're better at telling *your* parents about what's happening at school than this lot,' says Mr Angelo, unaware that he's repeating himself. 'Though of course we know what people your age are like – full of secrets kept from us boring grown-ups!'

Instead of answering, I just laugh, as if what Mr Angelo has said is the funniest joke ever.

'Oh my goodness! You girls must've been hungry,' Mrs Angelo remarks all of a sudden, staring at our practically empty plates that minutes before had been full of spaghetti.

What? Where did our spaghetti go? Is it swirling around in some parallel universe?

'Yes, we were,' says Sunshine to Mrs Angelo, with a meaningful flick of her eyes towards me. 'It was delicious, thank you. Is it all right if we leave the table?'

Suddenly I get it. Sunshine – or one of the angels – wants us to move on to something else. But what?

'We have homework to do,' Pearl adds very convincingly.

'We need Riley's help,' Kitt tells her foster parents, which is an even bigger fib – the angels know every answer to every question in every subject at school.

'Um, yes . . . that's fine,' Mrs Angelo replies, watching us make our way towards the hall.

Walking up the stairs, I hear Mr Angelo ask, 'Did one of the girls close the curtains? I was *sure* they were open.'

Hurrying silently after the angels, I wonder what's coming next.

We enter a loft room that's as blue as the sky in summer, with fat white duvets floating cloudlike on the three low, white-painted beds.

Once again I spend a few moments trying to figure out how this space can look more than *double* the size it was when my old friend Tia lived here.

'Close the door,' Kitt orders me firmly. I do, and I can't help letting my eyes settle on the chart by the light switch.

'What – what do Mr and Mrs Angelo think this is?' I ask, getting round to one of the questions that's been locked in my head this past couple of weeks.

Down one side, the chart has the girls' names; along the top there are the initials of all the skills. There are ticks and crosses and blank boxes yet to be filled. Pearl's line has the most crosses, always.

'They don't see it like you do,' Kitt says, as I watch her grab a pillow from the bed and toss it on the white-painted floorboards.

What does she mean? What do Mr and Mrs Angelo see? I spin my head back round to the chart – and gasp.

It's transformed into a hand-drawn poster. Pretty mismatching letters in various felt-pen colours spell out the cheery message, *Welcome to our home sweet home!*

I blink – and the chart is back.

I blink again – it's the 'home sweet home' poster.

Blink, chart; blink, poster.

Disbelieving, I do it a few times more, till Kitt grabs my attention.

'Coming?'

Kitt, Sunshine and Pearl are all in the middle of the loft room, kneeling on pillows. And there's one spare pillow – for me, I guess.

'Riley, we helped you just now,' says Sunshine, as I crouch down and join them. 'And it's your turn to help us, if that's all right.'

Oh, so Kitt *wasn't* fibbing when she said as much to Mr and Mrs Angelo a minute ago.

What's this all about? The three girls are holding hands, with Kitt and Pearl reaching out for me to complete the circle.

'Sure . . . how?' I say nervously, feeling Kitt's cool, firm grasp versus Pearl's delicate warm fingers.

'It's about the girl Marnie.'

At Sunshine's words, I feel a lurch of disappointment again, thinking about the party I won't be going to. But how can I let myself waste time over that? Specially when the angels are about to let me be part of something special, amazing, *magical* – I hope.

'At school, when we've been reaching out for Marnie, something is getting in the way,' Sunshine carries on. 'Some kind of interference.'

'Is it the red writing?' I suggest, feeling a little shiver.

'We don't know what it is. We only know we need to separate the strands; *then* we might be able to see more clearly,' Sunshine says.

'Tonight, we're going to try to seek Marnie's strand,' Kitt adds. 'If we can sense why she's fading, maybe we can begin to help her at the party on Saturday.'

'Do you understand?' asks Sunshine.

'Not really,' I say, wondering why we're in this linked circle. 'But what can I do?'

'Somehow the three of us aren't strong enough at the moment,' Kitt says, her eyes on Pearl.

Pearl bites her lip, unable to meet Kitt's eyes. Is she failing badly? But, even if Pearl's skills aren't strong, what can *I* possibly do?

'We'd like to use your energy, Riley,' says Sunshine. 'If you're all right with that?'

I find myself nodding stupidly, words slipping away – I'm so excited at the prospect of being a part of the angels' magic and not just someone for them to practise on.

'You *are* only human,' Kitt informs me, as if I didn't know. 'It might not work.'

'You're going to feel exhausted afterwards,' Pearl gently warns me.

'It's – it's OK, let's try,' I say, thrilled to think that I might be getting a close-up glimpse of the world through the angels' eyes.

'Are you ready?' Sunshine asks.

'I'm ready,' I say, taking a deep breath, and not feeling remotely ready.

'Then let's reach for Marnie.'

For a second, I'm just a nervous girl, kneeling on a pillow in a bright blue room.

But suddenly the pillow, the floor, the walls fall softly away, and my stomach lurches . . . till all is calm.

I'm weightless, warm and light, and floating in a blaze of brightness, connected to no one I can see, but by a vibration where both my hands should be.

'Marnie . . .' I hear the distant whisper of Sunshine's voice.

'Marnie . . .' Kitt echoes.

I wait for a third voice, but it doesn't come.

Instead, mismatching images begin to swirl around me. They're like the frantic colours painted on a waltzer car at the funfair one second, then it's as if I'm staring at a giant, translucent computer screen, endlessly scrolling through web page after web page.

126

Snatches of crowded classrooms, of teachers talking, of home, the sofa, Dad, of Woody with his wide grin, of red writing here, there, everywhere, of Dot in stripes, of Mum in a tea dress, of lorries thundering, car fumes on Meadow Lane, fresh air and breezes on Folly Hill, of Pearl scanning my face, searching, trying to understand me.

Of Pearl trying to get me to understand *her*.

Pearl.

She's in my head. *Now.*

'They're wrong; it's not her . . .' she's whispering.

The shock of it makes my eyes flip open, even though I didn't realize they were shut. I'm back in the loft, with my knees on the pillow, pins and needles prickling my legs.

Just for this second, I'm on my own here on the floor; the angels are beside me but still lost in their other world, eyes wide, blazing silver-white.

And in that second, as my heart thunders with wonder and confusion at what just happened and where I've been, I see a small something.

It's so ordinary that it doesn't seem right here.

It's a marble.

A glass marble, glinting from under Pearl's bed.

I might not have spotted it if the room wasn't filled with celestial light, so bright that it's making the marble seem to . . . to *pulse* with a metallic glow. But now the light is easing, fading, as the girls come back, their hands firm and still in mine. And, glancing quickly again under Pearl's bed, I see just a tiny, dark, round blob in the shadows.

Was it just a silly trinket she picked up and kept? Pearl is especially full of wonder at anything new. Only last week she danced and twirled in the fog that swooped in on Folly Hill. She and Dot ran around, trying to grab it, stuck out their tongues to taste it.

Yes, the marble is nothing.

Unless it's *something* . . .

'It didn't work, but thank you anyway,' Sunshine says to me, a gentle smile on her face. 'I'm sorry if we tired you out, Riley.'

As soon as she speaks, it hits me – a wave of exhaustion. I haven't felt this way – this worn out – since I had the flu or did forty lengths for that charity swim-a-thon at my primary school.

'I'd better get home,' I say, struggling to my feet, legs heavy and wobbly, treacle in my veins.

Kitt lets my hand go easily.

Pearl's clings a little longer.

Pearl.

As I stand up, I say quiet words of my own, even though I'm no angel.

Find a way to talk to me, I think in the privacy of my head, hoping she gets the message, impossible as that is.

Pearl smiles shyly, gratefully.

Hurray – I think she heard.

Straight into something serious

The usual rolling slideshow of bland school images is projected on the giant whiteboard suspended above the stage.

No one is paying the slightest bit of attention to it, as:

a) Friday morning assembly hasn't officially started yet so everyone's using it as chatting time, and
b) everyone's seen it so often it's beyond dull.

Me: *I'm* not paying attention because I'm still exhausted by whatever-it-was the angels did to me on Wednesday night at their house. I don't feel as bad as yesterday, though. Yesterday I was so tired I practically sleepwalked my way through classes. Thank goodness nothing tricky cropped up, like a test or something. And, hey, maybe the school spook was as tired as me; nothing weird went on for the first time this week. Maybe it's gone for good?

Then my sleepy head suddenly tunes into the whispering of girls behind me.

'She's a right snob.'

'I know she is.'

'But her party's going to be amazing, isn't it?'

'Yeah – can't wait to see her house. It's supposed to be pretty immense.'

'I heard it's *so* huge that as well as a living room there's this sort of *games* room with a snooker table in it and one of those TVs nearly as big as the wall.'

'I heard that too. And someone said it's so posh it's got a separate flat where her granny lives.'

'That's probably why she's a snob.'

'Yeah.'

I can see Marnie Reynolds's shiny, dark bob in the second row of chairs, close to the stage. Wonder what she'd think if she could hear the girls' conversation going on in the row right in front of me?

'What're you going to wear?'

'I am *so* going to wear my black skinny jeans, even though I can't, y'know, sit down in them.'

'Well, on Saturday morning I'm going to get this top I've seen – it's got this skull on it but made out of a pattern of flowers.'

'Nice. What are you doing with your hair?'

'I thought I could wear my hair up, in two little buns.'

'What – like that girl Kitt?'

'Yeah.'

'What, like Kitt who is sitting right behind us?'

The girl in the row of seats in front spins round and bursts into giggles of embarrassment when she sees the four of us.

'*Shame!*' says the friend who's pointed out how close Kitt is.

Wow, these girls are airheads. I'm glad I'm not going to a party that has guests like them.

'Morning, everyone!' booms Mr Thomlinson, the deputy head, as he comes striding into the hall and walks up a set of steps that lead on to the stage.

I'm about to pay attention (like we're all supposed to) when I hear a whisper in my ear.

'Riley . . .'

It's Kitt, who's sitting right beside me.

'Why do you care?' she asks silently, switching to quiet words.

'About what?' I ask out loud.

Miss Dunbar from the music department throws me a look that says *Shush!*

Out of all the angels, Kitt is the one who freaks me out the most, I think to myself (not for the first time) and hope she can't read *that* particular thought.

Pearl – and her ditziness – has always been the easiest to like, and I'm liking her more by the minute. And when Sunshine smiles my way it's as if something lights up inside me. But Kitt's long,

scrutinizing stares, her blunt way of talking . . . both of those can make a girl feel a little weirded-out.

The thing is, I *know* she's my friend. She might seem super-strict when it comes to skills, but on the trip to Wildwoods Theme Park it was *Kitt* who flipped out and lost her temper with Lauren Mayhew when she was being horrible to me. It was *Kitt* who let fly with the errant magic on the Haunted House ride, earning herself a big black cross on the chart in the loft of the house next door.

But that doesn't mean it's always easy being friends with her. Especially the last week or so; she's been the most serious I've ever seen her. Maybe she needs to take smile lessons from Sunshine.

'Why do you care about not coming to the party?' she asks me now, her voice in my head.

From snatches of conversation I've heard in corridors and classrooms, it seems like half of Year 7 have been invited to Marnie Reynolds's house. How do I explain to Kitt what it feels like when you're in the half that *hasn't* been invited? That even if you're not

that keen on the person whose party it is, it still makes you feel left out? That's probably *way* too girlishly complicated for a clear-thinking angel to understand.

And I'll miss watching Sunshine, Kitt and Pearl working their magic with Marnie. Well, maybe not Pearl, going by the strange psychic message she sent me on Wednesday night.

Uh-oh . . . Miss Dunbar is making warning eyes at me and pointing towards the stage.

'It's nothing. It doesn't matter,' I mutter to Kitt, as I turn to focus on Mr Thomlinson, who's now at the lectern. A huge version of the Hillcrest Academy logo appears on the whiteboard above his head – a stylized image of Folly Hill with the Angel on top.

'Seems like it does,' I suddenly hear Kitt murmur wordlessly back.

I don't have any time to figure out what she's on about; Mr Thomlinson is talking. And he's not starting off with his usual cheerful, welcome-to-assembly chat. He's fired straight into something serious.

'Well, this has been a very *trying* week so far, and I think we all know why,' he begins. 'There's been some extraordinary silliness going on around school, hasn't there?'

Rumbles and mumbles ripple along the rows, with everyone pretty sure what he's on about.

'These *messages* that have been appearing on toilet mirrors, by the fire alarm, out of the maths-block printer . . . they are not only ridiculous, they are wasting school time and resources, AND they're distressing some people.'

I automatically drop my gaze and look at the back of Marnie Reynolds's head, thinking of the asthma attack she had on Tuesday. Is she thinking of it too? She's scratching her head, ruffling up her neat hairdo. Maybe she's agitated at the memory. Or maybe – I grin to myself, thinking of Dot – she's got nits.

Though my grin vanishes when I realize what Mr Thomlinson says next.

'It's the work of something supernatural: a poltergeist, perhaps.'

More mumbles and rumbles erupt around the hall, with many shocked gasps and thrilled 'Yes!'s too. (I'm sure I heard Woody whoop. He would.)

I can tell everyone's taken aback, me included, by what our deputy head has just said. I turn round to gauge the angels' reactions, and see that they're sitting perfectly still, showing no emotion.

But *I* know their minds will be whirring, tuning in, seeking.

'*That* is what some frightened students are telling their teachers,' Mr Thomlinson carries on quickly, realizing the effect his words have just had. 'Of course that's absolutely, categorically *not* the case. I can assure you one hundred per cent that there are no *supernatural* powers at work in Hillcrest Academy.'

Mr Thomlinson holds his fingers up to indicate quote marks as he says the word 'supernatural', showing how ridiculous the very idea is. But it's too late for some of the audience, I can tell; they've only listened to the more dramatic part of his

speech and are now whispering frantically, like a nestful of agitated wasps.

And, personally, I'm not completely reassured either.

Not when I'm sitting beside three people whose amazing abilities would blow everyone's minds.

'It is *plainly* the work of one hoaxer, or a group of hoaxers,' Mr Thomlinson now booms, holding his hands up for calm, for quiet. Taking his lead, the teachers sitting round the edges of the hall start urging everyone to shut up and listen. (It's not really working.)

'This *has* to stop. NOW.'

Our deputy head pauses for dramatic effect – and the whole place erupts.

Wow.

He has no idea what's just happened.

Everyone in the hall is roaring, in either shock or excitement or both.

Cos projected directly above Mr Thomlinson's

head – in metre-high red, dripping letters – are five heart-stopping words:

TOLD YOU I WAS WATCHING . . .

The angels have been very quiet all the way home.

The angels are *exhausted*.

Ever since assembly, through every lesson, through break and lunchtime, they've scanned and searched, tried to tune in, tried to find truths, but nothing is clear.

'It's all static and noise,' Kitt grumbles, as we turn into Chestnut Crescent, far enough away from the prying ears of other Hillcrest students to talk openly.

'The strands were already tangled and hard to read,' Sunshine adds, shadows of tiredness under her eyes. 'Now everyone's nervous energy is like a *wall* to us.'

'But do you think there *is* some kind of . . . *force* occurring at Hillcrest?' I ask, not really sure what I'm asking, or if I want to know the answer.

'We weren't strong enough to find out today,' Kitt says glumly, staring down at the pavement as she trudges along.

'Should we ask for help?' Pearl suggests, bending to curl her fingers in the fluffy down of Bee's head as he pads beside us.

'From *me*?' I say, assuming – with a sudden twist of excitement in my tummy – that Sunshine, Kitt and Pearl might want to try channelling my feeble energy again. Not that it helped them on Wednesday evening.

'No!' Kitt says sharply, making me jump.

Eek . . . is Kitt cross with me, or Pearl? OK, it's Pearl. I can tell by the glare Kitt's throwing at her.

'We need to do this on our own,' says Sunshine, softening the sudden tension of the moment with one of her soothing smiles.

'Yes, but *how*?' Kitt asks irritably, showing a hint of the temper I know she has.

'We rest. We start again tomorrow,' Sunshine tells her, as she tosses trails of red-gold hair over her

shoulder. 'We use the party to concentrate on Marnie. The rest . . . the rest we deal with on Monday.'

Breaking things down, taking it step by step; it's the way Dad taught me to do my maths homework in primary school, when the fractions and decimals got all muddled and confused in my head.

Seems that piece of advice works whether you're a Year 6 pupil or a trainee angel.

'Riley! RILEY! Wait!' yells someone behind us.

We turn and see a grinning Woody, hurrying away from his Year 8 mates. A few of them call out stuff like, 'Oooo-OOOO-ooo – is that your girlfriend, Woodster?' and another takes a casual swing at Woody's head with a schoolbag. (It misses, luckily for Woody.)

'Are they *really* all friends?' Pearl asks me, looking at the boys dubiously. 'Isn't being mean a bad thing?'

Bee is as unimpressed with the Year 8s as Pearl, and barks his disapproval at them.

'Like I said before, boys have a strange way of showing they like each other,' I tell her, at the same time thinking that, in her own way, Kitt is being quite mean to Pearl at the moment. All the impatient snapping and those dirty looks.

I really wish, wish, *wish* I could get Pearl on her own to talk to her about that – as well as all the other stuff that whirls around my mind.

At that second, I see Pearl tilt her head slightly, as if she's just heard her name being called.

'Hey, wasn't that BRILLIANT this morning at assembly?' Woody pants, as he catches up with us, the spikes of dark hair flopping on his forehead as he slows his run.

'It was weird,' I correct him, not certain that 'brilliant' is the word I'd choose to describe those eerie words flashing up on the whiteboard.

'Yeah, but the way that visual came up just when Mr Thomlinson said, "This *has* to stop. NOW!" That was ace! I mean, *what* a fluke – you couldn't have timed it better.'

142

Woody's beside himself with excitement, as fired up by today's events as the angels are exhausted.

'You *did* take a photo of it, didn't you, Riley?' he asks me urgently. 'Tell me you did!'

'Yes, of course,' I say, nodding. My hands might have been shaking at the time, but I got the shot – which was a stunned Mr Thomlinson turning and staring up at the whiteboard screen, moments before a member of staff got to the remote and switched the projector off.

'Great. Good one, Riley. And, hey, I am *so* going to write the most amazing story about all this,' he says, practically punching the air.

'For *News Matters*?' I ask, frowning. 'But Daniel's already asked Ceyda to do it; she's the main features writer.'

The fact that he's only just joined the newsletter team seems to have gone straight over Woody's head. Even if he *is* amazingly full of ideas and enthusiasm, he can't just come storming in and expect to take over. I mean, *I* was nervous about my role as

newsletter photographer when he showed us that image on his phone. Ceyda's bound to feel the same if Woody tries to nick her job from under her nose.

'Yeah?' he says, disappointment draining his grin away, though it's back in a nanosecond. 'But what if I get a different angle on it? Something no one else has?'

'Like what?' I ask.

Woody doesn't get a chance to answer – there's a rugby-style hollering from behind and we all turn to see the Year 8s suddenly hurtling towards Woody, the boy with the bag twirling it round his head like a gladiator weapon.

'Uh-oh,' he laughs nervously. 'Better get going!'

He's only a couple of metres along the street before he remembers something and shouts it over his shoulder to me.

'Hey, Riley – got a message for you from Marnie in my class. She says you can come to her party tomorrow, if you want!'

Huh?

I'm about to shout a startled 'What?! *Why?*' after him but he wouldn't hear, not with the Year 8 lads deafening us as they roar by in pursuit. Bee's barking's not helping either.

Though I'm pleased to see one thing – the strap on the schoolbag circling the boy's head snaps, and the heavy bag flies round . . . and catches him flat in the face.

'He deserved that,' I murmur, pleased.

'Yes, he did,' Pearl agrees, and I turn and see that her eyes have a silvery sheen to them.

Kitt spots that too, and blasts Pearl with one of her intense glares. Even Bee's looking at her, but he's got his smiley dog face on as usual.

'So, that's good, isn't it? We can all go to the party together,' Sunshine says brightly. (Has she noticed the bag incident? Or is she just using her niceness to keep the mood light?)

Actually, I'm still a little too stunned to answer for a second; I don't know why Marnie would suddenly invite me, since she obviously thought I

was wangling an invitation when she was sprung by the angels on Wednesday.

But, before the second passes and I get a chance to collect my thoughts, Mrs Angelo wanders towards us, jingling car keys in her hand.

'Did I hear you use the P-word, Sunshine?' she asks, smiling.

Sunshine smiles back, but doesn't know how to respond. Angels, I've found, are like people from a different country, who've only just learned a language. They can see when something is obviously funny, but they're not great at deciphering jokes yet.

'You were talking about the party tomorrow?' Mrs Angelo tries again.

'Oh yes,' Sunshine says with a nod.

'Well, that's good timing. Because I'm taking you girls shopping right now for some party clothes. You arrived with practically nothing and you deserve something new. So come on – hop in the car!'

Sunshine, Kitt and Pearl seem slightly bemused and confused by the idea of party clothes, or *any* kind of new clothes. When they're not in school uniform, they only ever dress in variations of the same thing: dungaree dresses, black tights and lace-up boots for Sunshine; leggings and layers for Kitt; and T-shirts, denim skirt, stripy socks and glittery baseball boots for Pearl.

I think Mrs Angelo takes their hesitant smiles for breathless excitement, and turns to lead the way to the car.

'Here, Bee – are you coming for the ride as well?' she says, opening the boot for the dog to jump in.

And like the good (foster) daughters they are, the angels follow too, with only Pearl glancing back at me.

That glance – is it to let me know she heard what I was thinking a minute ago? Or is it a sign that reads *Help!* or *Now!* or *DO something!*?

Whatever it means, I get it. This could be that one chance, that one rare moment for me and Pearl to be alone together.

And, amazingly, my non-impressive mind comes up with a plan.

'Mrs Angelo,' I call out. 'I just remembered I have this really pretty dress I've grown out of. Pearl is smaller than me, and I said she could have it for the party, if it fits?'

Lies, lies, lies.

Except for the bit about Pearl being smaller than me, of course.

'Oh yes! It sounded so pretty,' says Pearl, astounding me with her ability to lie too. 'Can I stay and try it on while you go shopping?'

'Um, yes . . . but what if it doesn't fit, or you don't like it?' says Mrs Angelo, holding the back door of the car open so Sunshine and Kitt can slide in.

They're not sliding in; they're standing still, staring at Pearl, at me, wondering what's going on.

148

Even Bee is looking quizzically out of the rear window.

'If it's not right, then I have other nice stuff – T-shirts and cool . . . things!' I say, floundering in my fibs.

'Okey-doke, fine by me. See you in an hour or so, Pearl!' Mrs Angelo calls out, while waving Sunshine and Kitt into the car.

Sunshine and Kitt have no choice but to get inside, leaving me and Pearl waving them off.

Then we turn, look at each other and grin happily, with a little shyness thrown in there too.

'It's only us!' I say, hardly daring to believe it.

'Yes,' says Pearl, nodding her head and making her stubby plaits sway.

There's so much to talk about that I don't know where we'll start.

I guess I could just ask her how she's feeling; if Kitt being grumpy is bothering her.

Or I could find out why she thinks Marnie's not the girl who's stopped shining, and what she makes of the red messages happening at school.

Then I could ask her all the questions that've been buzzing around my head for ages, like:

a) how exactly the skills work,
b) what it feels like to have wings, and *hide* wings, and
c) can she remember anything of her life before she turned up in Chestnut Crescent?

I can even ask stupid stuff like why she collects marbles, I think to myself, remembering the glass ball I spotted under her bed.

Hey – we could chat about Mum, maybe.

Basically, we are free to talk with no one else getting in the wa–

'RILEY! PEARL!' yells Dot, clambering out of Dad's car with Coco in tow, fresh from school.

The two little girls dive-bomb us both, lunging hugs at us, as thrilled as if they hadn't seen us for a year.

'Hello!' Dad says cheerfully, thunking the car door shut. 'On your own, Pearl? Don't often see you without your sisters!'

'We're all invited to a girl in Year Seven's party tomorrow afternoon, and I said I'd lend Pearl something to wear,' I explain. 'Sunshine and Kitt have gone shopping with Mrs Angelo.'

'A party, eh? You'll have to tell me all about that,' says Dad, piling supermarket bags out of the back of the car. 'And, speaking of shopping, do you big girls fancy giving me a hand getting this stuff in the house?'

OK, so our time together will be delayed by a few minutes.

'Sure,' I say, grabbing groceries alongside Dad and Pearl.

'*We're* going to play dog shows with Alastair,' Dot announces, grabbing the front-door key from Dad and charging off to open up the house for us.

Dot's bedroom is directly above the kitchen, and as we dump the bags on the pine table we can clearly hear stomping small feet, plus muffled giggles and woofs.

'Before you disappear and do your fashion show, can you try and make some space in the freezer for this stuff, Riley?' Dad asks me.

'Course,' I reply, taking the pile of chilly packets he's passing to me.

As I yank at the stiff, frozen drawers and shove things around, I hear Dad chattily ask us a question about tomorrow.

'So whose party is this? And where's it happening?'

'It's a girl called Marnie. You don't know her,' I answer him, down on my haunches with my back to him. 'And her house is one of those fancy ones up by the golf course.'

I'm expecting him to say something.

Maybe ask if Marnie is in our class, or make a comment on how big those houses are round there.

But he says nothing.

152

And Pearl is saying nothing.

What's going on? Are they too absorbed in the excitement of stacking tins of beans on shelves or unpacking the toilet rolls?

I shuffle round – and freeze like a packet of fish fingers.

'What are you doing?' I ask, my heart lurching at the scene in front of me.

Dad is standing absolutely motionless, a box of Dot's favourite breakfast cereal clutched in his hand, in mid-air.

Pearl is staring at him, head tilted girlishly to one side, eyes solid silver.

'You want him to talk about your mother, don't you?' she says in a soft, breathy voice.

'Yes! Yes, of course! But what about Dot and Coco? They could come in any second!'

Pearl wafts a delicate white hand towards the ceiling, and I shut up. There's no sound coming from up there. Two little girls are playing a game of statues, whether they like it or not.

'I'm doing a spirit-lift. He's remembering something.'

Struggling to my feet, I go closer to Dad and see he's not *totally* still; his eyes are making tiny darting movements, as if he's watching something on a screen. And a smile is tugging at the corners of his lips.

'What's he remembering?' I ask.

'I'm not strong enough at this skill to see,' says Pearl, becoming paler by the second. 'But we'll find out *now* . . .'

She flicks her hand in the air, and Dad gives himself a shake and shifts his weight to his other leg. But his eyes are still hazy, hypnotized.

'I'd forgotten about the smell . . . it hits you as soon as you open the door of the shop . . .' he murmurs. 'All those scents mixed together! And the colours, the colours of all the flowers . . . There's Annie! Look at that huge bouquet in her hand. She's wrapping a wide yellow ribbon round the stalks, quick, quick, quick, and then the bow . . . I love the way she has her hair all piled up on top,

154

wisps trailing . . . She's smiling at me, and looks *so* pretty, even with that orange smudge of . . . what is it? The pollen from lilies, that's it . . . I love that smile – makes me glad I sneaked out of work to bring her lunch as a surprise . . . We can sit here eating our sandwiches, pretend we're in a tropical paradise . . . Turn the radio up so we can block out the sound of the traffic and the trains rumbling by . . . Oh, Annie, you are so beauti–'

The sound of the doorbell jars Dad back into the reality of here and now and breakfast cereal. From above there're some thumps and muffled giggles as the unexpected statue game ends.

'I'll get it!' I hear Dot roar, and there's a thundering of four five-year-old feet as she and Coco charge down the stairs and throw themselves at the front door.

'Is it me, or is it hot in here?' asks Dad, putting the box down and rubbing his forehead.

'It is a bit warm,' I agree with him quickly, although what he's just said has given me the shivers.

'Oh, dear – and *you're* looking pale all of a sudden,' says Dad, ushering Pearl to sit down on the nearest chair.

She *is* pale; pale and faint from the effort of doing two skills back to back after an already tiring day.

And now a horrifying thought hits me.

The *last* time she was this exhausted, Pearl couldn't stop what happened next. Back then, with a rustle and a crackle her wings had started to lift and show. But at least that was in the privacy of the girls' loos at school, not in my kitchen with Dad right there, two inquisitive five-year-olds close by and whoever's at the door!

'Look, it's . . . *everyone*,' Dot merrily announces, appearing in the room with Coco and waving enthusiastically for 'everyone' to follow her.

'Sorry, sorry, sorry,' says Mrs Angelo, as the kitchen is immediately filled.

Bee pads in and flops his head on Pearl's lap, while Sunshine and Kitt walk either side of Pearl and place a hand on each of her shoulders. I think

they're gently pressing down, pressing *something* down. Their hands are healing Pearl, infusing her with calm, keeping those wings from unfurling.

'You know, I'm such a fool,' Mrs Angelo carries on. 'We set off and then it dawned on me that I'd forgotten my credit card. And, since we had to turn back, the girls wanted to pop in here and give Pearl one last chance to come along with us!'

Sunshine and Kitt knew, didn't they? I can tell from Kitt's stony face. And I bet you a zillion pounds that she and Sunshine had something to do with Mrs Angelo *forgetting* her card.

'Actually, I'm glad you *did* turn back,' says Dad. 'I don't think Pearl's feeling too well.'

'Is she going to be sick?' asks Dot, eyebrows shooting up with excitement.

'No, I don't think so,' says Dad, trying – and failing – to shoo her and Coco away.

'Really? Oh, Pearl – look at you!' gasps Mrs Angelo. 'Let's get you home.'

There's a flurry of activity as everyone helps Pearl to her feet and leads her towards the front door.

'Hope she feels better!' Dad calls out, as the angels, Mrs Angelo and Bee make their way down the garden path.

'Hope you don't barf!' Dot yelps helpfully.

'Thank you,' I say in my head, hoping Pearl can pick it up.

She does.

She turns.

She mouths a word at me over her shoulder: *Tomorrow.*

I understand the word, but not the meaning.

Tomorrow, as in Marnie's party? Or tomorrow, as in us getting the chance to talk alone together?

I guess I'll just have to wait till tomorrow to find out.

Ready or not?

Dad gave me a present when I started at Hillcrest in September.

'Now that you're at secondary, you're old enough to let yourself in and be alone in the house occasionally,' he'd said, passing me a set of keys dangling from a cute letter 'R' key ring.

Nice idea, Dad.

But it never works out like that. Our house is always full, or at least it feels that way, cos of Dot skedaddling around, pretending to be a tiger or a fairy or a vampire shark or whatever.

And, if I get home from school first, I usually only have five minutes or so of me-and-only-me time before either Dad or Hazel arrives back from picking up Dot (and often Coco) from primary.

But – yay! – this morning is different.

Hazel's working an early shift at the hospital and Dad's had to go into his printing shop for an hour or two, even though he doesn't usually work on Saturdays, cos of some rush job that's needed for Monday. Dot's gone with him, cos she loves the fact that she can photocopy all of her scribbly drawings there. (She took them into her class last time and tried to sell them for 10p each. She came home with 22p and a squashed fudge.)

So today the house really *is* all mine.

'What should I do?' I ask Alastair, who's hunkered on the tartan blankie in his dog basket.

His surprisingly sensitive eyes (drawn on by me in marker pen) seem to look up, but he doesn't answer (no surprise).

I suppose I could laze and watch TV. Have an epically long bath. Try clothes on and decide what to wear to this afternoon's party. Try and figure

out – like I did all last night – what Pearl meant by 'Tomorrow'.

BING-BONGGG!

Or answer the door.

I only open it a little way – I don't need the postman to see my super-comfy but slightly ratty pyjamas.

'Hello, Riley. Are you ready?'

Pearl is standing on the doorstep, smiling at me. Maybe she's hoping that I'll think she looks better than last time I saw her, but she doesn't really.

'Ready for what?' I ask.

Does she mean the party? But it's only 10 a.m. We don't have to be at Marnie's for hours, I think to myself.

'It's not the party. And I'm feeling good, honest.'

I stare at her, my mouth flapping as much as my baggy pyjama bottoms. I did *not* say that stuff about the party out loud.

'Can you read *everything* that's in my mind?' I suddenly ask, freaking out at the idea of Sunshine,

Kitt and Pearl having had open access to my mind all these weeks.

'No . . . it's only when people are stressing. They have a sort of purple haze surrounding them.'

Pearl wafts her hand around her head to indicate where this *haze* is.

'I'm *purple*?' I say, turning to look at myself in the hall mirror, which is dumb, I know, since I'm not looking through angels' eyes.

'A tiny bit mauve,' says Pearl. 'I shouldn't have looked.'

'It's against the rules, anyway, isn't it? Aren't you supposed to save your powers for important stuff?'

I don't mean to go all preachy and Kitt-ish on her. But, even though I'm grateful for the glimpse I got of Mum last night, I'm still uncomfortably aware that breaking those rules is going to wear Pearl out.

'*You're* important to me,' says Pearl, biting her lip.

'Am I?'

'Yes, you're listening to me. Sunshine and Kitt aren't.'

OK, OK. It looks like we're going to have that conversation that I imagined would happen yesterday – before Dad, Dot, shopping and spirit-lifting got in the way.

'You'd better come in,' I say, waving her inside.

'No – we need to go. I only have a little time. Are you ready?'

Pearl smiles hopefully at me again.

She is speaking in angel riddles.

But I'm an ordinary girl who needs to change out of her PJs before she does anything.

In the shopping centre across town, Sunshine and Kitt will be trying on clothes, as Mrs Angelo looks on approvingly.

Up on Folly Hill, Mr Angelo will be throwing sticks for Bee to catch.

Pearl – under strict instructions from her foster

parents – is cuddled up in bed, having a long lie-in to get her energy back after the funny turn she had yesterday.

Only she's not, obviously.

Pearl spotted an opportunity when it landed at her angelic feet. She waited till everyone went out, then got dressed and sneaked over to mine – with a plan.

'Where, uh, are we going exactly?' I ask for the fourth time, as I hurry to keep up with Pearl.

'Sunshine and Kitt think I do it all wrong,' she murmurs in reply, as we stride downhill through the winding neighbourhood roads, heading towards the west side of town (I think).

I'm beginning to wonder if Pearl will be able to help with all my questions. She slips and slides away from even the simplest – like where we're going and what her plan actually is.

'They say I have to do the skills *their* way, but I'm not so sure,' Pearl carries on distractedly.

'Because you think they're wrong about Marnie?'

I ask her, giving up on directions and trying to follow her train of thought.

'Mmm . . .' She nods, bounding along the pavement fast, in a hurry to get to wherever we're going.

'But why do you think that? Didn't you go to her the other day in the playground? You saw she was in trouble.'

'I'm sure it was just a catch, Riley,' says Pearl, her gaze straight ahead. 'I sensed that someone was ill. And when I got to Marnie her shine was weak – and *that's* what Sunshine and Kitt saw.'

'So . . . is she fading or not?' I ask, unsure what she's telling me.

'Not enough to need our help. Everyone's shine fades when they feel ill. But Sunshine and Kitt – they've decided it's her and that's that. Even though it's not clear, not with the other stuff that's getting in the way at school.'

'What other stuff?'

'The . . .' Pearl lifts her hands and shakes them

165

around, her white-blonde eyebrows knitted in a frown as she tries to explain.

'Interference?' I suggest, remembering the word that Sunshine had used sometime in the last few days.

'Yes!' says Pearl, nodding. 'But today at the party we can get close to Marnie. There'll be no interference. *Then* they'll see that I'm right.'

'Is *that* what you meant by "Tomorrow"?' I ask, noticing the traffic's getting busier as we leave the suburban streets behind. 'Or is it . . . what we're doing now?'

'I meant the party. This – this is extra. This is for *you*.' She suddenly smiles mischievously, turning her gaze towards me.

Though her eyes aren't their usual pale grey at the moment – they're getting more intensely blue by the second.

'Pearl, what's going on?' I ask her, my heart thumpitty-thumping.

'You can see what you need to see, Riley,' she tells

me, 'and Sunshine and Kitt will see that I can use the skills in a different way and *not* lose my glow . . . We're here!'

What do I need to see? What is her glow? I don't ask, because I've just realized where we are.

On the pavement opposite a row of shops.

It's not the trendy or busy side of town, but plenty of people are passing, stopping, looking in windows, thanks to the position of the railway station further up the road.

A man is coming out of the newsagent's; another is walking into the betting shop. A teenage girl is on her phone outside the chemist's; a woman with a buggy is staring at kids' clothes in a shop called Little Ones. Two old ladies are sitting chatting animatedly inside a cafe.

And then I remember *another* old lady, *another* catch . . .

It was when the new family moved into Tia's old house next door. I'd gone for a walk up Folly Hill with Dot (and her trusty stick on a lead) and come

across the strange-but-interesting Angelo sisters by the statue. Of course I didn't know what catch was at the time, but it's what happened when Kitt suddenly foresaw the old lady walking over the brow of the hill. Unfortunately, there just wasn't enough time for Kitt to stop her from tripping over Dot and Alastair as they ran (and dragged).

I remember the old lady's hair, puffed and backcombed like candyfloss. I could smell the cloying sweet scent of hairspray as I helped her up.

I remember the quizzical look she gave me as she studied my face.

I remember her saying, 'You know, dear, you look *exactly* like someone I used to buy flowers from. What was her name? *Annie* – that's it! Annie's Posies, that's what the shop was called. Used to be right by the station. Do you know her?'

I remember lying and saying no, I was so shocked to hear someone talking openly about my mother.

'Which one was hers?' I murmur, frantically

scanning each shop in the parade, as if they'll give me clues.

'*That* one.'

And, with no regard for traffic, Pearl steps out into the road. Luckily, the stream of vehicles is moving slowly.

'Sorry! Thanks!' I gabble, holding my hand up to cars as we wend our way to the opposite pavement.

Pearl knows where she's going. Her glittery baseball boots walk past the woman with the buggy and we are through the glass-panelled door of Little Ones.

All around us are pine cots and wicker Moses baskets, painted wooden toys, dainty pastel Babygros and cute patterned bedding. The shop has an old-fashioned feel, with a thick polished counter at the back.

No one is behind the counter right now. The one member of staff I can see is showing a customer how to fold and unfold a brightly coloured buggy.

'Come,' says Pearl, and she takes my hand and draws me towards the back of the shop. 'Feel . . .'

What I feel is stupid, ridiculous, self-conscious. What will people think? Why would two twelve-year-old girls be in here? Specially when they're stroking a counter, for goodness' sake.

I'm not going to do it.

I'm going to wriggle my hand away from Pearl's surprisingly tight grip and get out of –

Here . . .

She's here.

Or maybe I'm *there*.

The smell. The scent of all those flowers.

And there are flowers everywhere, every colour, every type. SO many flowers . . . How does she remember all their names? How does she know which will go with which?

'Oh, Annie! Those are *beautiful*. Thank you,' says a woman's voice, but I can't quite make her out – it's hazy round the edges.

'My pleasure,' says my mother, in view now that

she's come out from behind the counter with the beribboned bouquet in her hand.

Mum is pretty, even prettier than she is in the photo. Her fair hair is bundled back into a messy ponytail. There's no tea dress today, just jeans and a checked shirt worn over a pale green T-shirt ... which in turn is worn over a big bump.

Me.

'Not long now, eh?' the other voice says. 'Thought of names yet?'

'We're playing around with a few,' Mum says with a smile, staring down. 'Riley's the favourite at the moment.'

'Riley! Well, that's unusual,' says the other voice. 'I look forward to meeting you, Riley.'

The woman talking leans forward to touch Mum's tummy, and I recognize her. The hair ... it's not as puffy as it becomes when she's older, but I still recognize her from Folly Hill, that day back when —

171

'Can I help you?'

The flowers are gone.

Mum is gone.

A woman with a badge that reads *We LOVE your LITTLE ONES* is talking to us.

She'll get no sense out of Pearl; my friend is standing with her head tilted, a far-away look in her vivid silver-grey eyes.

And I don't know how she'll get any sense out of *me* cos I'm so shaken by what I've seen, where I've been in these last, amazing seconds.

'I – I . . .'

'Riley?'

At the sound of my name, spoken by a kind and familiar someone, I turn round.

'Mrs Sharma!' I gasp, seeing my old form tutor. She's holding the handle of the brightly coloured buggy, her tiny baby cuddled in a baby carrier on her chest.

'What are you doing in here?'

I've always liked Mrs Sharma. She didn't need

to have angelic powers to see I was struggling after Tia moved away. She might even have been able to help me more, if her baby – little Raina – hadn't been born quite so soon. (Mrs Sharma going into labour when we were both accidentally locked in the caretaker's office was, er, interesting.)

'We . . . um . . .'

Excuses rattle round my brain, then fizzle away under the beam of Mrs Sharma's warm, encouraging smile.

Maybe I should risk telling the truth.

'I think this used to be my mum's shop, years ago,' I blurt out.

Wow. It feels scary – and *good* – to tell.

Like some kind of weight is lifting off my shoulders. I feel lighter, brighter.

'Really?' says Mrs Sharma.

I can see it in her eyes; she's thinking of my school files, of the entry that mentions the fact that my mum died. Form teachers always know that kind of

family stuff. If she'd been around when the Angelos had started at school, she'd have read about them being fostered.

She reaches out and pats my arm. 'It must be strange for you coming here and seeing –'

'Sweetheart?' the sales assistant interrupts her, talking directly to me. 'I don't think your friend is feeling too well.'

Uh-oh. Pearl. Her skin is so pale it's practically translucent.

Maybe it's time for lies now.

'It's OK. She gets like this when she hasn't eaten . . . and she hasn't had breakfast today,' I say quickly, linking arms with Pearl. 'We'll go and get some food. Bye!'

'Bye, girls,' Mrs Sharma calls after us.

'I'm sorry,' Pearl says faintly, as we get outside into the fresh air. 'I wanted you to see her, but I don't feel too good now.'

'Don't be sorry,' I say hurriedly, spotting a bus coming that will take us close to home.

174

As I flag the bus down, I make a real effort to block my thoughts.

I don't want Pearl spotting any shimmering shades of purple.

Cos my emotions are in a total tangle right now. There's guilt, at Pearl putting herself in possible danger, doing what she's done today on my behalf.

But there's also so much joy that I could skip and whoop.

When I stood in my PJs in the hall this morning, wondering what I should do with myself, I had no idea I'd end up seeing my mum living, breathing, smiling . . .

Well, almost.

And, after all the years of nothing, *almost* feels pretty wonderful.

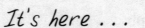

It's here . . .

'Big kids' parties are rubbish,' Dot announces.

That's pretty harsh, considering she wasn't even invited to Marnie's party. But here she is, in the sheeny-shiny nylon princess dress she insisted on wearing. Even Alastair is dressed up, with a sparkly ribbon tied round his driftwood neck.

Dad's rush job at work this morning turned into a nightmare, and looking after Dot turned into a nightmare for him too. She was getting bored, and he found her drawing smiley faces on the newly printed business cards of a firm of solicitors.

So I found myself babysitting.

'Shh,' I tell her now. 'That's not a very nice thing to say, is it?'

'Well, it's not a very nice party, is it?'

Actually, I think I agree with her. The house is amazing – as huge as everyone said it would be – but there's a funny atmosphere here.

Me, Dot and the angels have wandered around all the crowded downstairs rooms, and it feels like people are acting either grumpy or kind of crazy.

I guess *I'm* grumpy cos of Dot – much as I love her – being dumped on me. Sunshine and Kitt (especially Kitt!) seem grumpy with Pearl, since they sense she's been up to something, even if they're not a hundred per cent sure what it is.

But lots more people here seem grumpy. Lauren Mayhew and her buddies Joelle and Nancy are standing in the hallway, with faces as sour as fresh lemon, whispering and scowling over every girl, boy, outfit and hairdo that arrives through the front door.

And Marnie Reynolds, she's over by the sound system in the games room, and she's not looking too thrilled either, even though this is her party.

I guess I should go over to her and say thanks for the invitation and sorry for the unexpected five-year-old. But getting across the games room isn't going to be easy, because of all the craziness.

A bunch of girls are shrieking and spinning each other round to the music, bumping and crashing into everyone anywhere near them.

A couple of lads who've been playing snooker are having a pretty full-on argument. (I'm going to have to cover Dot's ears if it gets any more heated.)

Someone has put the giant telly on and is flicking madly through the channels, which is doing my eyes in.

A bunch of boys have opened a window overlooking the garden and are pretending they're going to chuck someone out of it. (I think it might be Woody – he really has *terrible* taste in friends.)

'We should go to Marnie,' says Sunshine. She

looks amazing. Under her dungaree dress she's wearing a silver spangled T-shirt. Mrs Angelo's added a dab of silver glitter to her cheekbones too, and her long, lapping waves of hair are pinned back with a cluster of clips in the shape of silver stars.

'Shouldn't we just go and find some crisps instead?' Dot suggests, holding on tightly to Sunshine's hand while she clutches Alastair with the other.

'It's important that we speak to Marnie,' Kitt says to her. Kitt has new leggings – still black, but with a blue-beaded trim round the ankle. It's the same deep blue of her new baggy T-shirt, made out of some kind of shimmering material.

'There's no point – it's not her,' says Pearl. She might not have been on this morning's shopping trip, but Mrs Angelo bought her a new dress and bag anyway. The bag is made of a dusky rose velvet, with a strap long enough to be worn across her chest, across the pretty, embroidered bodice of the short white smock. The smock would be totally cute on Pearl, if she didn't look paler than the colour of the dress itself.

'What's not her? What's not a point?' Dot pipes up, staring at her big-girl pals and probably wondering why nobody's smiling.

'We don't know that till we *seek*,' Kitt snaps at Pearl, but switching to quiet words now.

'You have to trust me; she's not the one, I'm sure!' Pearl silently stands up for herself.

'What's happening, Riley?' Dot asks me, just as confused by this new, wordless weirdness going on.

'Stop it,' Sunshine urges her sisters in her own unspoken way. Same as me, she can plainly see that one angel's anger and one angel's exhaustion equals carelessness – and danger.

'Hey, why don't you check the tables in here?' I bend down and say to Dot. 'I bet you there'll be a bowl of crisps on them!'

Hurray for the promise of potential crisps. Dot lets go of Sunshine's hand in a nanosecond and disappears into the mayhem.

180

As I try (and fail) to see where she went, I notice that the bunch of boys by the window have given up on attempting to chuck Woody out. I've just seen a cushion whirling through the air, landing, I suppose, somewhere on the big lawn out there. I hope they don't do the same to any crisps they come across, or Dot might go feral and bite their ankles.

'But we *can't* trust you,' I hear/see Kitt say sharply as I turn back to my friends. 'You're doing things wrong, Pearl. Your powers are ebbing. Your glow is going. And you're not listening to any of us!'

Is Kitt including *me* in that? She must be, otherwise she would've said 'either of us'.

But that suddenly makes me cross. Pearl is so sweet and has been so kind to me, and I don't want Kitt making me part of *her* problem.

'Look,' I lean in and whisper to Kitt, since a whole sentence of quiet words is beyond me. 'You're not giving Pearl a chance. She did the most amazing spirit-lift and spring on my dad last night and this morning she did a telling, all by herself!'

I had hoped that Kitt would be impressed; Sunshine too. But, from the sudden glower on Kitt's face and the saddened frown on Sunshine's, I can tell that's definitely not happened.

'Oh, Pearl . . .' murmurs Sunshine, as if Pearl's just been to the doctor and had a terrible diagnosis of some kind.

Pearl blinks hard – she has tears in her eyes.

'Do you realize the trouble you could be in?' Kitt asks out loud.

'Leave her alone!' I surprise myself by saying. 'Pearl has been really kind to me. Can't *you* be kind for once?'

I don't get a chance to see Kitt's reaction – Dot's scream cuts through all the music and roaring and chaos.

'NOOOOOOOOOOOOOOO! RILEY!!'

It's coming from the direction of the window.

The boys – the boys are all laughing. For a

horrible, horrible second I panic that they're about to throw my little sort-of-stepsister out of the window. But as soon as I get over to them I see that they've done something that – in Dot's eyes – is nearly as bad.

'It's just a stick!' one lad cackles, when he spots the ferociously protective look on my face. I glance around and see they're *all* cackling like manic Cheshire cats, beside themselves at the funniness of the moment.

They don't seem to notice that Dot is crying her eyes out, sobbing at the fact that someone has torn her pet from her arms and thrown it out of the window.

I push aside the boy who talked and peer down into the garden, trying to locate Alastair.

But someone is already down there searching. Woody.

'Come on,' I say to Dot, grabbing her hand. 'We'll get him back.'

Hustling her out of the room and into the

cavernous hall, I spot a short set of stairs heading downwards and assume they'll lead us into the garden.

Sure enough, there's a glass-panelled door that's already open.

'Any sign of Dot's . . . pet?' I call out to Woody, not really sure how to describe Alastair to anyone outside the family.

'Here – *ouch*! Here's your dog,' says Woody, stepping out from the depths of a red-berried holly bush with Dot's hunk of driftwood in one hand and a bleeding scratch on the other.

'Alastair!' Dot yelps, running to grab and hug and dance around the garden with her rescued mutt.

'Thank you,' I say to Woody, passing him a clean but scrunched-up tissue from my pocket.

'No worries.' Woody grins, dabbing the tissue on to his hand and then – in true boy style – lifting it up to inspect the blobs of red on the paper.

'Your friends are idiots,' I say, nodding my head

towards the now-empty window, though the pounding music and accompanying hollering is still going on, I can hear.

'They're not my friends – they're just in my class,' Woody says with a shrug.

'So your proper mates are those Year 8 boys I've seen you with?' I ask, my dislike for those lads probably written across my face.

'Nah, not really,' he says with another shrug. 'I just hang out with them on the way to school. Try to make them laugh and whatever.'

'So who *are* your best mates, then?' I ask, trying to picture him with anyone in particular at school. I guess I've seen him chatting to loads of people, always goofing around, but not with any one boy, or group of boys.

'Hmm,' says Woody, rubbing his chin and raising one eyebrow, cartoon style. 'Which of the *hundreds* of people do I choose from?'

I can't help but smile – he's pretty funny and likeable.

'Well, Marnie Reynolds must like you, since she invited you,' I point out.

'She invited everyone in our class, and a whole bunch more besides, so I'm not so special,' he grins. 'But Marnie's all right, once you get to know her.'

'What does that mean?' I ask, wondering if I'll find out something that might help the angels with their mission.

'Everyone thinks she's a snob, cos of where she lives.'

'And because she acts a bit snooty too,' I point out.

'Nah, she's all right. It just takes her a while to warm up and trust you. She said at her primary school, lots of people pretended to be her friend, just so they could come and check out her *posh* house.'

OK, I suppose that fits with what she said when the angels sprang her. I suppose I shouldn't take her coolness so personally. Though I still don't know why she changed her mind and invited me to her party.

'Wait – if Marnie's so funny about people wanting to be friends with her for the wrong reasons, then why did she want to have this party in the first place?' I ask, the thought just occurring to me.

'I think it was just to get back at her mum,' says Woody.

I scrunch my nose up – the universal sign of *Huh?*

'Well,' Woody carries on, hopefully about to explain it better, 'Marnie came into class last Monday and said her mum was going away on a business trip this weekend. Her mum does it a lot, she says, and always promises Marnie she'll cut back on trips and work stuff – only she never does.'

'So Marnie was just mad at her?' I say.

'I guess so. So next thing she's telling everyone she's having this party. But I think she regretted it about five seconds after she said it!'

Sympathy swirls in my chest for Marnie. We've all got angry and said things in the heat of the moment – *Like me with Kitt upstairs a minute ago, I*

wince to myself – but not all of us will have to spend the rest of the weekend scooping peanuts out of the snooker-table pockets and gathering tossed cushions from the flower beds.

'Isn't her dad around?' I ask.

'Think they're divorced. There's just her nan – who lives in there.'

I turn round and see a set of French doors and a bunch of windows, in what must be the basement of the house. The granny flat I heard about.

'She must be one deaf old lady,' I say, wondering how anyone can ignore the noise thundering above her.

'Marnie says she's at the hairdresser's. Hope her appointment lasts a few hours!' Woody jokes.

'Riley,' a little voice interrupts us now. 'Can we go, please? I don't like this party. It has bad boys and no crisps.'

That sounds like a reasonable description of the party to me. I'm about to say yes, when Woody leaps in.

'Aw, don't go! It could get better!' he says, sounding genuinely disappointed.

Somewhere in the house up above, I hear a crash, a tinkle of glass, accompanied by groans and hoots of howling laughter.

'I don't think so,' I say with a wry smile.

'Just stay a little while longer – I really want to speak to you about working on the school newsletter. It's important!'

'Riley, I *really* want to go . . .' whines Dot, in that shrill five-year-old way that makes your ears twinge.

'Dot – I'm pretty sure I know where some crisps are,' Woody suddenly tells her. 'If we can find you some, can you let your sister stay for just a tiny bit longer, so we can talk?'

Dot thinks. Dot frowns. Dot speaks.

'Are they *really* nice crisps?'

'REALLY nice crisps!' Woody promises her. 'Coming?'

'They'd better be nice,' grumbles Dot, taking

Woody's hand and stomping off like a Disney princess in a very bad mood.

'Don't go anywhere, OK?' Woody says over his shoulder.

'OK,' I say, wondering what he wants to talk to me about.

I hope he doesn't think I'll be able to persuade Daniel and the others to let him write the main piece about the mysterious red messages. I only know the newsletter crew well enough to say 'Hi' and 'Do you like my photos?' so far.

Speaking of photos, my hand automatically goes to the camera in my bag. I brought it along this afternoon, wondering if Marnie would appreciate me being her unofficial party photographer. But the way things are going I have a feeling she might prefer to forget all about it once she finally gets rid of everyone – whenever *that'll* be.

'Riley?' It's Pearl, who's just pattered down the stairs and appeared in the doorway, passing Woody and Dot on the way.

If this was a month or so ago, Marnie's party might well have had a Halloween theme, and Pearl would have fitted right in – as the ghost of a 1960s girl in her mini smock dress.

I didn't know it was possible for anyone to look that pale without layers of theatrical make-up and dramatic, spooky lighting.

'Where are the others?' I ask Pearl, as she steps into the garden and pads over the lawn in her sparkly baseball boots.

'They're hovering around Marnie,' she says, shivering a little in the watery, wintry sunshine. I'm kind of chilly myself.

'Won't they want you with them?' I say, wishing I hadn't promised Woody – and Dot – that I'd wait here for them. I fold my arms over my chest, as if that'll hold the heat in.

'Maybe. But I don't have enough energy to help,' she says with a small smile.

The small smile worries me. It's as if she's trying to hide something.

'What can I do?' I ask quickly. 'Do you want me to get your coat, so you can get warm?'

She is shivering, from head to spangly foot.

'Do you need to go home?'

I suddenly think of Dad – his print shop isn't far from here. Maybe I should give him a call. He could do that thing with the car, where you can flip the flat part of the boot up and have two extra seats. We'd all fit in then. Dad wouldn't mind. And I'm sure Woody could wait, and we'll have that newsletter conversation on Monday at school.

My hand is now scrabbling in my bag for my phone instead of my camera.

But Pearl seems to ignore all my questions and simply says, 'I think they might be right.'

'About Marnie, do you mean?' I whisper, leaving my phone where it is for a second and motioning Pearl to move behind the dense green expanse of the holly bush, so we're away from any prying eyes in the house.

'No – about me doing things wrong. I think the

glow *is* going,' says Pearl, sounding scared, I realize with a shock. 'Can I show you something?'

'Uh, yes,' I reply, nervously watching as she pulls something out of her small velvet bag.

It's a package of some sort, a silky handkerchief the blue of a summer sky, gathered up at each corner and tied with a thin silver thread.

'Do you want to see my skills, Riley?' she says in a small voice. 'For real?'

'But I – I've seen you use them, I've *felt* you use them,' I fumble around with a response, not sure what she means by *for real*.

All those mind-blowing questions I have about the angels? Maybe it *is* better if I don't ask, don't know.

Cos right this second, I'm suddenly a little bit frightened, and I'm not sure I really want to see what Pearl is about to show me.

Whatever's inside the soft, silky package in her hand . . . whatever it is, it's *moving*.

'But we haven't shown you our *personal* skills,' says

Pearl, pulling at the silver string. 'And I've seen you have questions in your head about how they work.'

I'm hardly daring to move, to breathe.

'So I thought I would take mine to show you today. But, Riley, when I checked them just now . . . there's something very wrong!'

The thread falls away, and the silk material opens up like blue petals.

And in the middle, held in Pearl's now-cupped hands, are eight tiny spheres, turning in tiny, jerky movements against each other, glowing with the faintest fluttering light. At first I think they're made of glass, and then I see that they're soft, like gel, as they squash and rub up against each other.

What exactly am I looking at?

'They used to be so much brighter, Riley!' Pearl whispers to me, anguish in her voice. 'As we gain experience, our skills glow more strongly and spin faster. In time, the glow is so bright, the spinning so

fast, that it will be just one bright, intense ball of light and then . . .'

'You'll have . . . qualified?' I suggest, using a word so normal it sounds pathetic for the wondrously strange phenomenon I'm staring at.

'I thought helping you would make the glow stronger, but it's got weaker – same as it does if we use errant magic,' says Pearl, staring down in dismay at the stuttering, stalling twirling beads of glass or gel or whatever it is they're made of. 'Sunshine and Kitt said we always have to work together, but I didn't want to. And now this is happening . . . and I don't know how to tell them that *one* of my skills has gone altogether!'

Eight spheres. Of course, there should be nine – one for each of the angels' skills.

I see fat tears start falling, soaking darkly into the blue silk. Pearl is now shaking with fear as well as cold.

'But what does it mean? Why are you so worried?' I ask her.

'Take a photo of me, Riley!' Pearl suddenly insists, lifting her gaze and staring at me with her watery, pale grey eyes.

'What?' I say, confused.

'Do it – then you'll see!'

But I won't see anything, I think, grabbing my camera anyway. Only a warm beam of light – I have the evidence in that photo of all three angels on my pinboard in my room, even if no one else looking at it would understand what they were seeing.

Holding up the camera, I fix Pearl in the viewfinder and press.

Click!

Now looking at the image in the display, I have to stop myself from gasping. There's hardly anything there – a scene of a winter garden, with the faintest gleam of something that you'd hardly notice, that you might mistake for a blur of a passing moth.

'Do you think I'll disappear completely, Riley?' asks Pearl, an edge of sadness and panic in her voice.

Pearl has helped me see something I'd never have dreamed of the last couple of days. But I can't help her – I'm only made of flesh and blood and human uselessness. But I know two special people who can and will.

'Quick,' I tell her, folding her hands round her precious package, to keep it safe. 'We have to find Sunshine and Ki–'

'Riley!' comes an urgent shout. 'Are you still down there?'

It's Woody. I step out from behind the shelter of the holly bush and look up, trying to locate him. OK, *there* he is, leaning out of an open window on the first floor. A bedroom, maybe? There's no sign of Dot.

'You've *got* to see this!'

'What?' I call up, not in the mood for party gossip, if that's what this is about.

Woody grins down at me.

'Riley, it's the red writing – it's here, in the house!'

As if I didn't have enough reasons to shiver.

197

Surprise, surprise

It must be a spare bedroom – there are no personal pictures hanging on the walls or special objects on the chests of drawers. It's a bit like a really nice hotel bedroom, only with a pile of coats dumped on the bed.

And, of course, the scribbled red message scrawled on the mirror.

SUPRISED TO SEE ME?

'Take a photo, Riley,' Woody demands excitedly. 'Daniel's going to love this, isn't he? Wait till we tell him. He's *got* to let me write this story now! None of the rest of the *News Matters* team are here . . . only us!'

I take one snap, ignoring the sight of my own shaking reflection in my favourite denim shirt, black tights and shorts, then nervously move closer to take another.

Pearl is nearby; I've sat her down on the bed. I want to sneak a look at her, see what she makes of the message, but it's hard with Woody here with us. And, with her own fading, how can she even begin to seek anyway? I wouldn't want her to, in case it made her weaker than she already is.

'Listen, you know when I said I wanted to talk to you, Riley?' Woody babbles, frantic with nervous energy and oblivious to the fact that Pearl is poorly. 'It's just – well, if Daniel *does* let me write this feature, can you help me? Write it, I mean?'

'But I'm the photographer, not a journalist,' I remind him.

What's he on about? And hold on, where's Dot? Weren't they supposed to be going on a crisp hunt together?

'Look . . . the thing is, I have dyslexia. Really, pretty *bad* dyslexia, OK?'

I forget about Dot for a second – Woody sounds so on edge, agitated.

'OK,' I say, lowering the camera, glad to step away from the strange message. 'But so what? Lots of people have that.'

'Yeah, maybe,' Woody says with a shrug, 'but *those* people might have classmates who are cool about it, instead of the bricks-for-brains lads *I've* been landed with in Y7A.'

'Do they give you a hard time?' I ask, suddenly concerned for him.

'Hard? Only hard like concrete. Or cement, maybe.' Woody can't help but joke, since that's the way he seems to deal with everything. 'So I'd just like a chance to show them that I'm not some loser they can laugh at.'

I'm not seeking – obviously – but suddenly I get a sense of how lonely Woody must have been since he started at Hillcrest, trying to be the joker among people that aren't at all nice to him.

200

His gaze falls to the floor, his expression and real feelings hidden behind his flopping spikes of fringe.

I'm trying to think what to say, how I can let him know that I *get* it, that I understand what it feels like to be alone in a crowd, that we might have that in common.

I reach out to touch his arm.

And then I see something that makes me pull my hand away.

On Woody's fingers . . . red smudges. Like a pen that's leaked.

I quickly glance back up at the writing on the mirror. I didn't read it properly the first time cos I was so shocked to see it.

SUPRISED TO SEE ME?

Surprised, but minus the 'r'.

Now I *really* get it.

This message, all the messages at school last week – they weren't the work of a poltergeist, or even some mean hoaxer. They were done by a boy who's sad and frustrated, and hoping a bit of

attention might change the way people see him. Oh – and a boy who's not so good at spelling. Especially when he's rushing to write, so he can show me the message before I leave the party.

'Woody – where is it?' I snap.

'Where's what?' he answers, taken aback at the edge of urgency in my voice.

'It's in his back pocket,' says Pearl. Her gaze is dropped to her lap, where her hands are clasped together. But even from this angle I can make out the silvery crescent moons under her trembling white eyelashes. She's tuning into him.

Before I can feel self-conscious about doing it, I reach behind Woody and pat both his jeans pockets – and whip out the thick whiteboard pen I find in one of them.

'Oi! Oh . . .' Woody protests, then lets his voice drift to a mumble when it dawns on him that there's no point in arguing with me.

'This is seriously *bad* – rub off that writing before anyone sees it,' I order him, wrapping the leaking

red pen in another scrunched-up tissue and shoving it to the bottom of my bag, to be dumped as soon as possible.

'OK, OK! So yeah – I did it, Riley . . . but *please* let's tell Daniel and everyone that the rest of it's real?' Woody begs me, not making a move towards the mirror. 'I just want to do something important, like write this story. It's not as if it's hurting anyone!'

He'd planned to do it all along, it dawns on me. Last Monday morning on the way to school, Woody told me he had a great idea for the *News Matters* meeting. I thought the red writing replaced whatever that original idea was, but it turns out the red writing *was* the original idea.

'Don't worry, I'll get your coat for you,' a voice calls loudly.

Help! It's Marnie. She's close, just out on the landing.

'What colour is it?' she shouts to someone who must still be on the floor below, waiting to leave, to get away from the craziness of the party.

Before I can think what to do, she's here.

Marnie's dark shiny bob swings to a standstill as she stops dead in the doorway, taken aback to see the three of us in the spare room, and then shocked to see what's plainly scrawled on the dressing-table mirror.

'Look, it's just a joke,' I fib quickly, not knowing how else I can explain away this mad moment.

But Marnie doesn't see it as a joke. Her hand flies to her chest, which begins to heave, labouring for breath.

'Marnie – the writing, it's nothing weird, I promise. *I* did it! It was me, not some spook!' Woody blurts out, seeing the impact his prank has had on his classmate.

'Here, sit down,' I say urgently, pulling Marnie over to the bed, where she hunches over, desperately trying to regain control over her breathing.

Pearl immediately reaches out to stroke Marnie's head, letting the warmth run through her fingers.

OK, that should begin to help, I think, my heart and head pounding.

'What's she doing?' bleats Woody.

'A kind of head massage,' I lie hastily, glad to see Pearl's eyes have fluttered shut, hiding the telltale silvery sheen they've taken on. 'It's to relax her.'

'Oh. Right,' Woody grunts.

I *think* he believes me, but I'm more caught up in what I've just spotted nestling in Pearl's lap. Her silky blue bag of secrets. She needs to hide that away, *quickly*. But, as she's so caught up in soothing Marnie right now, I'll deal with a couple of other hugely important things first.

'Woody – wipe that off *now*!' I order him, pointing at the mirror while I wonder where in the house Marnie would keep her asthma pump.

Woody finally moves, rapidly turning the long sleeve of his T-shirt inside out, doing his best to rub the glass clean. 'It was just meant to be exciting – something people would talk about. I didn't mean for anything bad to happen!'

As he works at making his smeared words disappear, I turn back to look at Marnie, whose wheezing is worsening, her lousy party becoming more of a disaster by the second.

Then I raise my eyes to see that Pearl's lips are moving.

'*Riley* . . .'

Quiet words. This is important; I need to concentrate.

'*Riley, it's him* . . .' Pearl is whispering, her voice meandering into my head.

'*It's him . . . it's him* . . .'

Wait. Is she saying what I *think* she's saying?

It's *Woody*? Woody is the person the angels have been searching for?

This is crazy! *Beyond* crazy. But there's no time to think about it now, however crazy and important and mind-blowing it is.

'Marnie?' I say urgently, kneeling down in front of her. 'Where's your inhaler? I'll go and grab it for you.'

'There's one – one in the basket – on the hall table.'

'I'm on it,' I tell her, swiftly rising to my feet.

But I'm *not* on it.

Fear has suddenly rooted me to the spot.

The blue silk bundle in Pearl's lap – she didn't fasten it properly. The silver string has slackened, the soft material unravels, the softly glowing 'marbles' slither from their nest, flopping and dropping on to the floor.

Moving super-fast, I grab the silk square, then crouch and grab up every small sphere, aware of how cool and soft and *trembly* they feel as I wrap them up safely again.

'What're those?' I hear Woody ask.

'Lucky charms,' I mumble, putting a hand on the bed to push myself upright. Then it hits me. I picture another bed, or at least the space under it. I *know* where Pearl's lost skill is.

'Those don't *look* like lucky charms,' I'm suddenly aware of Woody mumbling.

My heart begins to pound madly, as I see what he's seeing.

No, no, *no*!

Pearl is unfurling . . .

'Pearl? Please don't!' I beg uselessly, knowing that my friend is beyond exhausted, beyond stopping what's inevitably happening.

I stuff her precious package into the pocket of my black shorts and step in front of Woody, hoping to block his view.

But how can I hide *this*?

With a rustle and a flurry, up they come: two arcs of white feathers at first, then with a final creak and crackle they're there – two great wings, gently swaying at her back.

Marnie sees nothing, hears nothing, locked in her own battle with her breathing.

But Woody is losing it, crashing back against the drawers, as terrified as anyone he frightened with his red-writing messages at school.

I have no idea what to do.

Luckily, the two girls who've quietly stepped into the room, closing the door behind them, do. They'll make this right, I know.

It begins straight away.

I notice that Marnie's breathing is now as stilled as the rest of her, same as Woody is frozen, perched awkwardly on the edge of the chest of drawers, his hands held up in front of him in fright.

'Help us, Riley,' Kitt murmurs in my mind, wrapping her arm round my waist.

Sunshine is holding her other hand, while reaching out to place her palm on Pearl's wing.

Instinctively, I rest my own hand on Pearl's, which is still stroking warmth into Marnie's bowed head.

We're joined, the four of us.

And whatever feeble energy I can offer them I give it gladly.

The brightness begins . . . the heat intensifies . . . the world vibrates gently . . . then *whoosh*, a coolness comes over us all.

But my mind is muddled, cloudy with the effort.

Where are we? What point has the memory rewind taken us back to?

If it's *before* Marnie's asthma attack, then Woody won't understand the implications of his unsettling messages, and know why his pranking *has* to stop.

If it's *after*, then Marnie will know that Woody was to blame for it all. And, stupid as Woody's been, it won't help mend his shine if he gets expelled.

Coolness.

Coolness . . .

I blink, and find I'm standing beside Woody, stuffing his pen in my bag. Pearl is sitting on the bed, her gaze in her lap, silver crescents of light behind her white eyelashes – but no wings in sight.

So *this* is where we start again.

'Don't worry, I'll get your coat for you.' Marnie's voice drifts from somewhere outside the room, but she sounds further away than last time.

It's up to me to make the most of these unclaimed

few seconds, manipulated and squeezed in by Sunshine and Kitt.

'Here's the deal,' I say to Woody, as I run over and frantically wipe away the words on the mirror. 'You promise me one thing, and I'll promise you two.'

'What?' he mumbles, frowning, puzzled.

'*You* promise me you won't do any more of the red writing, ever again. Promise me.'

'But –'

'And if you do,' I say urgently, aware of the sound of Marnie's footsteps on the stairs, '*I* promise I'll never tell, and that I'll help you write a really great cover story for the newsletter.'

Woody's face softens, his shoulders sink a little, and I see the tension that's always been in him ease.

I don't think anyone's offered to do something good for him in a very long time.

'What colour is it?' I hear Marnie shout, outside on the landing.

'I promise,' he agrees, nodding quickly. 'But what could we write about that would be really cool?'

'*You,*' I tell him, as Marnie swings into the room with a surprised 'Oh!' at the sight of us.

'We're just getting our stuff,' I say quickly, grabbing up Pearl's pink duffle and shoving it round her shoulders. 'Thanks for inviting us to your party, Marnie —'

'Marnie! MARNIE! SOMEBODY WANTS YOU!!'

'Oh no, they haven't broken something else, have they?' Marnie sighs, turning on her heels and heading back down the stairs.

'Give us a hand,' I ask Woody, looping one arm under my fragile friend's elbow. 'Pearl's not feeling great – I need to get her home.'

'Uh, sure,' says Woody, gently taking Pearl's other arm and helping her out of the room and along the corridor. 'What's wrong with you, Pearl?'

'Migraine,' I answer for her. Pearl nods along to

my lie, though there's a chance she doesn't even know what one of those is.

'Er, Riley,' Woody mutters, sounding unexpectedly shy.

I hope he doesn't want any more details about Pearl's 'migraine'. I'm starting to get a headache myself with all this lying.

'What did you mean about the article being about *me*?'

Phew, he doesn't.

'Tell you later,' I say, probably sounding more blunt than I mean to.

It's just that I need to get Pearl out of here and back to Chestnut Crescent quickly – *and* find Dot. There'll be plenty of time to concentrate on Woody. It's what the angels will be doing a lot of from now on, I suspect, with my help, of course.

Speaking of Dot . . .

'*Right*, madam,' I suddenly hear an elderly but firm voice drift up from the bottom of the stairs. 'How about we start with my friend Dorothea?'

'*Princess* Dorothea Madeleine,' my sort-of-stepsister corrects her.

Woody, Pearl and me reach the top of the stairs and I tentatively peer down.

Sunshine and Kitt are sitting on the bottom step, surveying the scene in the hall.

The scene is of shamefaced Marnie standing in front of an old lady, who happens to be holding Dot's hand. Lots of people are hovering around, gawking.

'Well, I just found *Princess* Dorothea Madeleine outside in the front garden using our house phone. Any idea who she belongs to?' the old lady continues.

I can't quite make her out from this angle.

'Riley!' squeals Dot, spotting me and giving me a cheerful wave, the receiver still in her hand.

'It's OK – she's with me,' I call out, trying to get down to the hall and claim her as quickly as I can without rushing Pearl. (Sunshine and Kitt glide up towards us, taking her from me and Woody.)

'Well, that's one question answered, I suppose,' says the old lady. She must be Marnie's nan, I guess, home from the hairdresser's to find a house gone haywire – partygoers everywhere and stray princesses on the loose.

Now I'm in the hall, with the front door standing wide open, and I can see Marnie's nan more clearly. Her hair is puffed up, freshly backcombed and sprayed into something resembling candyfloss.

My tummy lurches. I know her. Or at least I've seen her once before. Twice, if you count the telling Pearl did for me this morning when we were in my mum's old shop.

'Of course the more *important* question is,' she's saying to Marnie, 'what on EARTH is going on here? What am I supposed to tell your mother?'

'Oh, Nana!' Marnie cries, bursting into tears and throwing herself at her grandmother. 'I wish they'd all go!'

'There, there, I'll take care of that,' the woman says, softening, hugging Marnie close.

Over Marnie's shoulder, she smiles as she sees Dot hugging me happily.

Then her smile fades into a more quizzical expression.

Uh-oh, time to go . . . and luckily Kitt must have rushed upstairs and grabbed all our coats.

'Thanks again,' I mumble in Marnie's direction, and make for the front door.

'Hold on, sweetheart,' says Marnie's nan, reaching out a hand to bar my way. 'Haven't I seen you somewhere before?'

'Don't think so,' I say swiftly, hoping her memory isn't good.

'Oh, I was sure I must've,' she says, sounding doubtful. 'It's just that you look *so* like someone I used to know. Someone who died. Listen, you're not . . . you're not *Annie's* daughter, are you?'

I ran away last time she asked me something similar, but I'm getting tired of running from the truth.

Taking a deep breath, I get ready to say 'Yes' . . .
when someone else does it for me.

'Yes, yes she is.'

Dad.

Dad is in the doorway, taking a wary step inside.

'I phoned Stuart!' Dot says proudly. 'I couldn't
find you, Riley *or* crisps, and the party was boring,
so I called him to come and take us all home!'

I want to kiss her. I want to run to Dad. Cos
sometimes it feels good to be rescued by angels, but
it's pretty special and wonderful to be rescued by a
member of your own family too.

Especially when that family member is smiling,
finally, at the mention of Mum's name.

Wouldn't you like to know . . .

I'm running, racing, breathless.

Nearly there.

Nearly at the very top of Folly Hill.

Nearly at the statue.

It's as if she's watching us coming, me and Woody.

'Made it – *I* win!' I call out, slapping my hands on the marble plinth a split second before Woody does.

'You must've cheated,' he pants, flopping his back against the ice-cold stone.

'How could I have cheated?' I protest, even though I know he's just teasing.

It feels good to be up here, gasping lungfuls of chilly air, watching clouds tumble across the December skies. We've been at my house all morning, working on our project together. Lately, the angels have quietly, little by little, secretly strengthened his shine, but the homework thing is *my* way of helping Woody. Every Saturday morning we've decided he'll sit at the kitchen table with his new laptop, and I'll talk him through any school stuff that trips him up.

But he's finding it's much easier now that he doesn't have to write with pens or pencils. I'm so pleased that the SENCO teacher came up with funding for the laptop for him after our joint article appeared in the newsletter.

And, of course, Woody's buzzing from the sudden fame. You wouldn't believe how many people have come up to him, asking him questions about his dyslexia, telling him about their own hassles. (At the last *News Matters* meeting, I joked that we should develop a new section, a problem page called 'Woody's Wisdom'. He threw his balled-up, muddy football shorts at me for that.)

'Do you ever miss her?' he asks, suddenly serious.

At first I think he's talking about Mum.

She's been on my mind a lot recently – Dad's too.

But we're taking baby steps. I loved listening to the short conversation he had with Marnie's nan at the party, hearing them talk about their shared memories of Mum, of her flower shop. Dad didn't go into detail, and he got us to leave pretty soon after the old lady mentioned how sad she was to hear what had happened to Mum. But something small started that day, and though Dad still doesn't seem to want to talk about her with me yet, I did find a little box containing a few more photos of Mum left on my bed one day (and Dad found a little thank-you note in his sock drawer later).

Actually, I'm going into town with the angels this afternoon. It'll be mobbed with Christmas shoppers, but I don't care – I really just want to buy a nice album to put those photos in.

'Riley? Did you hear me?' says Woody, rubbing his hands together to keep them warm. 'I said, do you ever miss Tia?'

I glance down the hill as we both watch the angels coming in our wake, Sunshine and Kitt swinging Dot between them.

Sunshine smiles my way, probably sensing that I'm thinking about them all – which instantly reminds me to put my mental block in place so she can't see any more, even if what I'm thinking is all nice.

Well, *virtually* all nice. I still feel a bit guilty that I accused Kitt of being unkind at Marnie's party. The truth is I wouldn't have been at Marnie's party at all if Kitt hadn't been kind enough to place a strange little thought in Marnie's head that day in assembly. A strange little thought that made her scratch her head, wondering why she hadn't got round to inviting me. (It wasn't nits, sadly.)

Pearl is taking her time, I notice, bringing up the rear with Bee. It's been a couple of weeks since the

party and Pearl is still a little pale, a little weak. But she's a lot stronger and brighter than she was – which is thanks to me, I'm pleased to say, and our little secret.

(I mean, what Sunshine and Kitt don't know won't stress them. If they'd found out that Pearl had misplaced her ninth skill, let it roll under her bed where it could've been vacuumed up and lost forever, they'd have been *beyond* mad with her. Thank goodness I remembered the 'marble' I'd spotted the evening I sat on the angels' loft floor.)

'Yeah, I miss Tia sometimes,' I tell Woody, rubbing the silver locket at my neck. 'But I'm pretty lucky with my new friends.'

'Me too,' says Woody.

I feel my face go pink – and that's not something I want Woody to see, or I'll never hear the end of his teasing.

'Fancy cloud-gazing?' I suggest, flopping down on my back on the frost-hard ground.

'It's freezing! Are you crazy?' he asks, leaning over me, staring down.

And the strangest thing happens . . . it's as if miniature white feathers are fluttering by his head, as if the angels are subtly showing themselves to him, giving him delicate, soft hints that they're around him, helping him.

That can't be true, though.

I mean, there's plenty I still don't know about my neighbours next door, and plenty I'd still love to ask them (and, yeah, I'm still a little *scared* to ask). But one thing I'm sure of – to them, I'm special.

I'm the only one who knows who and what they really are, and my lips are staying zipped up for sure.

'Why are you laughing?' Woody grins, as the feathery whiteness drifts down, speckles of cold landing and melting on my face.

'Cos I'm Riley Roberts, I'm crazy and I'm happy. *Whee!*' I yell, sticking my tongue out and letting the snowflakes land on it.

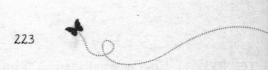

'What *is* this stuff?' I hear Pearl exclaim in wonder, as Kitt and Sunshine gasp, and Dot giggles.

'*You* lot,' Woody says with a shake of his head, 'are *all* mad. What kind of weirdness is going on in Chestnut Crescent?'

Wouldn't you like to know, Woody? I smile to myself, watching as he sticks his tongue out and joins in with us crazies . . .

Make your own friendship bracelet

Friendship bracelets are great fun to make and
even better when you make one with your best
friend! Just follow our step-by-step guide and you'll
have a unique gift – one that's really simple,
but really special to you both!

1. Choose three colours of embroidery thread or old wool – pick any colour
combination you like. Why not check out the 'What colours mean' chart below
and pick colours that represent your friend's character?

2. Take two strands of each colour.

3. Tie a knot at the end of the six strands and separate the different colours
from each other.

4. Get your friend to hold the knotted end of the bracelet and start plaiting the
three colours together – cross the two strands on the left over the two strands
in the middle, and then do the same with the two strands on the right.

5. Repeat this until the bracelet is long enough to go round your wrist,
then tie a knot at the other end.

6. Snip off any straggly ends and tie round your wrist.

7. Now repeat the above to make a second bracelet for your friend!

What colours mean

Red: Enthusiastic   Orange: Friendly   Yellow: Cheerful
Green: Chilled   Blue: Loyal   Purple: Imaginative
Pink: Sweet   Brown: Kind
White: Honest   Black: Deep thinker

www.karenmccombie.com

Create a Friendship Collage

A collage that's all about you and your friends —
that's got to look great on your wall, right? Or why don't
you make one in secret, as a surprise for someone?
Of course, there are websites where you can create an
online collage, but there's nothing like getting a bunch of
photos and images and snipping, sticking and gluing
them together by hand!

1. Decide on the theme.

What do you and your friend(s) like to do together? Share a hobby?
Watch movies? What makes you laugh, squeal, drool? Decide on your theme —
and you're ready for Step 2 . . .

2. Grab some photos.

The snaps you use should be of you as well as your friend(s), or group shots
of you together. Choose a variety of sizes and shapes, as well as photos taken
from different times of your life. (If you don't want to use the ACTUAL photos,
copy them on a printer and use the copies instead.)

3. Flick through some mags. or the internet.

Browse through magazines or online to select headlines or images
or even just fun words that represent the theme of your collage.
Rip out the pages or print out your favourites to use. You could also look
for a quote from a film or book that you both love, or maybe even
a phrase you always say to each other.

4. Get creative.

For a cool collage, cut each photo into an interesting shape. If you have a photo of you and a friend, for instance, cut round your bodies and discard the background. Or maybe stick your heads on to a star made out of silver foil, or transplant yourselves on to a funny background, like a scene in Harry Potter!

5. Add the words.

The words and phrases you've picked from magazines or online should be a variety of sizes, shapes, fonts and colours.

6. Get gluing!

Stick the larger images on to a poster board (from art shops) or just some cardboard, and then paste other images around them. Try to cover every area of the backing board with either a photo or words. Remember: you can get clever with your background too – if you don't want to have just one big rectangle, you could cut it into a circle, or even a chunky letter from the alphabet, like the first letter of you or your friend's name.

7. Final touches.

Got any tickets from shows you've been to together? Even tickets from things like swimming or ice skating are nice last-minute additions. And scrabble around for some craft stuff to add sparkle, like bits of ribbon or sequins. Even buttons look cute!

8. Tah-nah!

Your collage is ready. Stick it up on your wall, or present it to your friend. And don't forget – you can always update it by adding a new photo to it now and then.

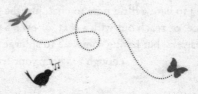

www.karenmccombie.com

How to be an Everyday Angel

The Angelo sisters use their magical abilities to
help Riley — but you don't have to be a real angel
to help others! Check out these six ideas for
how to be an everyday angel . . .

1. Say it, don't think it.

A girl you know has a nice new hairstyle. A boy in class who's usually
annoying has done a great drawing. Your best friend was really good fun today
and made you smile when you were grumpy. You might fleetingly notice and
think about stuff like that, but how about saying something out loud?
Come right out with a compliment? Giving someone a bit of praise can boost
their self-confidence big time. And make you new friends!

2. 'There, there . . .'

Feeling ill is pants. If your friend is off sick with flu or whatever,
be aware that she will be feeling
a) ropey,
b) mopey, and
c) like she's missing out on the fun that you and your other friends are having.
So get yourself round to hers after school or at the weekend, armed with chat,
chocolate and maybe a favourite magazine. Or, if she's infectious,
gather your friends to shout, 'Get well soon!' down the phone to her.
That should help her smile through the snot!

3. Be an ace listener.

You can tell something is bothering your friend, but she keeps saying she's
'fine'. Maybe she doesn't want to talk in front of others, so how about
arranging to have a little time to chat, just the two of you? You can suggest it
face to face, or reach out with a text, or even a note. You might not have all the
answers, but having someone to splurge her feelings to might be
enough to cheer your friend up.

4. 'If you liked that, you might like this . . .'

Start a book group. And don't just invite your BFs... ask girls you don't
know so well, who you know like reading. You might turn people on to books
they wouldn't have ever tried before. And, for people who are a little shy,
getting together to talk about books and stories and authors is a great way to
be sociable. (Don't forget the biscuits — you ALWAYS need biscuits
at a book group!)

5. Make homework not suck.

It's easy to get stuck on homework, especially with creative subjects
like writing or projects. But being in a group, bouncing ideas around,
can really flick a switch on in your brain!
So suggest get-togethers to help each other out — but lay down the rules too:
1) be nice (no poo-pooing what people say),
2) be encouraging (you'd want the same) and
c) no gossiping (you can save that for later, once the homework is done!).

6. Mad makeover time!

If a friend is feeling a little flat or fed-up, get silly with an over-the-top
makeover. Invite her round, blast some music on, and try out a ton of different
hairstyles and make-up looks on her. Get her to pose in the mirror,
or catwalk up and down the bedroom. It'll be even more fun if you get
her to do the same to you!

www.karenmccombie.com

Riley's story continues
in . . .

angels
like
me